The Missing Wife

ALSO BY ROGER SILVERWOOD

The MISSING WIFE

ROGER SILVERWOOD

JOFFE BOOKS

Revised edition 2025
Joffe Books, London
www.joffebooks.com

First published as *Choker* in Great Britain in 2004

This paperback edition was first published
in Great Britain in 2025

Cover art by Nick Castle

ISBN: 978-1-80573-180-1

ONE

It was two o'clock on a cold November morning. The sky was as black as an undertaker's hat. A man hurried out of a house carrying a carpet on his shoulder. The roll was about eight feet long. He rushed up to a car with its boot already open and dropped the carpet into it. It hit the floor with a dull thud. He glanced around and then quietly pressed down the lid of the boot, jumped into the driver's seat and drove swiftly away.

Half an hour or so later, the car was miles from the house. The driver pulled off a country lane and slowly made his way down an unmade road. Wild elderberry bushes brushed the car doors as the driver pointed the bonnet towards a beck that led into an open reservoir. The car stopped at the water's edge. The driver doused the lights and turned off the engine.

The noise of the thrashing of the water, forcing its way through rocks, made a thunderous din exaggerated by the loneliness and darkness of the night.

The man opened the car boot and took out a pair of wellingtons. He changed into them, slinging his shoes into the car. The sound of a breaking twig followed by loud, repetitive shrieks from a pheasant, as it flew disturbed from under a bush, sent his heart racing. He drew in a quick breath and froze for a few seconds, his back pressed hard against the side of the car, his pulse thumping. He stopped, looked around and listened. He fished in his pocket for a handkerchief and wiped his forehead and cheeks. After a few seconds, he made a determined lunge into the boot and struggled to get a suitable hold of the carpet roll. Eventually, he managed to gather it up and manoeuvre it over his shoulder, then he walked into the torrent. It was cold. The water was soon up to his knees. The load on his shoulder interfered with his natural balance. The noise of the water pounded loudly in his ears. Ever present was the sensation of someone watching him. His hot sticky hands were quickly chilled in the spray. He readjusted the carpet roll and, while doing so, lost his step on a stone in the rushing water. He staggered momentarily. At the same time, something lifeless, white and slim, slid out of the carpet into the chilling water. There was a slight splash. The current immediately took the body downstream away from the bank, the water lapping over the slim white stomach and blonde flapping hair as it glided away and disappeared into the dark, frothy water. He stared after it for a second. His mouth tightened. He swallowed with difficulty. The gushing water drummed even louder in his head. He hesitated for a second and then swiftly hurled the limp carpet off his shoulder into the water and bustled back to the car.

* * *

Detective Inspector Angel growled something unintelligible as he firmly closed the door painted with the words, 'Chief Constable.' Although a heavy man, he bounced down the stairs of the police station as fast as the youngest policeman in the station. He strode out along the olive-green corridor and stuck his big pug-shaped nose into the CID room and surveyed the occupants.

'Watson,' he growled at a very slim Asian boy of about eighteen who was dressed in a smart dark suit. The young man looked up from a desk, puzzled.

'Find DS Gawber, and bring him, yourself, and three teas into my office, pronto.'

The boy stood up promptly, closed a file of papers he had been reading and said, very precisely, 'I'll do exactly as you say, inspector; but you *know* very well that my name is Cadet Ahmed Ahaz.'

Angel stood looking at the dark, earnest young man for a second. He nodded and smiled. 'I know, lad. No need to get so touchy.'

Then the big man swept along the corridor into his own small office. He slammed the door shut and slumped in the padded swivel chair behind the cluttered desk. It groaned at his weight. He clasped his hands behind the back of his neck and pressed his head backwards. He let out a long sigh and arched his aching back. After a while, he shuffled the papers around his desk, sighed and stood up. He looked into a mirror on the wall. He peered more closely into it, and with one finger pulled down the fleshy part of his cheek under one eye. 'What you need is a holiday, lad,' he said to himself. After a few seconds he added, 'And a bottle of Hennessy and a packet of fags.' He slumped back down in the chair.

It had been a long day and he had little to show for it. The crime figures were up. They were always up. The chief constable was complaining. He was always complaining. His eyes caught the clock on the wall in front of him. It was four o'clock. He'd be going home soon to his wife . . . and *she'd* be complaining. What was it *all* about?' He shuffled papers around on the cluttered desk in front of him again. He glanced briefly at several letters, but one after another put them down without assimilating what they said.

There was a knock on the door. It opened and there stood Ahmed with a tin tray depicting a grinning pageboy advocating the virtue of some patented beef cube as a hot, refreshing drink, with three plastic cups of tea perched contemptuously across the illustration.

Angel swept three empty cups from the top of his desk into the wastepaper basket on the floor and pointed to a clear space for the tray. 'There,' he said to the young man.

A fresh-faced man of around thirty appeared at the open door. 'You wanted me, sir?'

It was Detective Sergeant Ron Gawber.

'Come in. Shut the door. You're harder to find than the Loch Ness monster.'

Angel looked towards Ahmed. 'You stay as well. You might learn something. Take a pew.'

The inspector pointed to the tray of tea. 'Help yourselves.'

Angel noisily slurped the hot tea, then put it down on the desk. 'I've just had a right bellyful from him upstairs.'

'Oh, what's getting at him?' Gawber asked, sipping the tea. 'Is it this off-licence robbery?'

'That, *and* the shoplifting, *and* the burglaries, *and* the drugs, *and* the rape case, *and* the inspection that's coming up, and . . . well, you name it!' He put the plastic cup down. 'Are you getting anywhere with this job?'

'We've finished the house to house and nobody saw anything.'

'They never do.'

Angel's thoughts stayed with the meeting he'd just had with the chief constable. He rested his hands on the desktop. 'Have you got a cigarette, Ron?'

Ron Gawber smiled. 'You know I don't smoke, sir.'

'Ah!' he snarled. Then he glared at Ahmed. 'I know it's no good asking you.' He turned away. 'Fags are getting as scarce as underpants on "Top of The Pops." '

'My mother does not approve of smoking,' he replied politely.

'And you always do everything your mother says, don't you?' Angel said testily.

'Yes, sir,' Ahmed said, subdued but not ruffled.

Angel had given up smoking quite recently, but at times like these he missed the nicotine and the business of doing something with his hands. He reached up and clenched them behind the back of his neck and arched his back.

'I could go to the shop and get some for you, sir,' Ahmed said brightly.

Angel softened. 'No thanks, Ahmed. I'm not supposed to smoke, anyway,' he said. Then, banging his fists on the desk, he fumed, 'These doctors nearly drive you mad. I'll bet you in a year or two, someone will come out and recommend that everybody should smoke from being a week old. My grandfather smoked forty fags every day of his life from being eleven years old and it never did him any harm.'

Ron Gawber smiled sympathetically. 'And I bet he lived to a ripe old age.'

'He died when he was forty-nine,' Angel said sullenly.

Ahmed smiled.

There was a knock on the door.

'Come in,' Angel bellowed.

It was a young, uniformed police constable. He stuck his head through the open door.

'Sorry to bother you, sir. There's this man at reception who says he's lost his wife.'

'Lucky devil,' he said quietly, then he leaned forward gripping the arms of his chair and said, 'Well, what does he want us to do about it? This isn't the lost property office!'

'I know, sir, but—'

'There's people going missing every day. Glad to go missing some of them. You know the drill, constable. What are you bothering me for? Tell him to try their milkman, or her mother's, or the Salvation Army or . . . Maybe she's joined the Foreign Legion — I hear they're taking women now!'

The young constable flushed at the verbal torrent.

It was Gawber who came to his rescue. 'Is there some special reason why you're reporting it to the inspector?'

Grateful for an opportunity to say what he came in to say, the young constable entered the office and closed the door. 'Yes, there is, Sarge. He's sort of — untidy — like grubby, needs a shave, dishevelled — you know what I mean.'

'Send him to the cleaners then lad,' Angel said impatiently.

The constable shook his head. 'And it's not like him, sir,' the constable said urgently. 'I *know* him. It's Sir Charles Millhouse, our MP.'

It was as if a bomb had been dropped in the little office. It wasn't that anybody normally took precedence over anyone else in Bromersley police station, but this MP was just about the most conspicuous MP in the House of Commons. Always immaculately dressed. Always ready to give an irreverent opinion on an irrelevant subject of the day or night. Always involved with high profile glamorous women and the big political and business set. Always seeking publicity. Always wore a top hat on Budget Day, in keeping with age-old tradition; and unfailingly wore a carnation in his buttonhole. This wasn't your average man off the street!

Angel leaped to his feet. 'Why didn't you say so, lad. You're like the Millennium Eye. You go round and round without going anywhere. And when you do stop you're back where you started from. Get back to him. Wait two minutes and then show him in here.'

The constable left hurriedly.

Angel put the unfinished plastic cup of tea on the tray and handed it to Ahmed. 'Take this, lad. Go and do something useful. See if you can break that computer again.'

'It wasn't me, sir,' Ahmed muttered as he sailed off through the door bearing the tray.

He turned to Sergeant Ron Gawber and said rapidly, 'See what you can do about digging up a witness for that shop job. If you could find the weapon it would help. I'll ring you later.'

'Right, sir.'

'And close the door on your way out.'

Angel hurriedly scraped all the papers on his desk together and pushed them in a drawer. He looked around the room and put a chair back against the wall.

He dusted off some invisible cigarette ash from the front of his suit, fastened one button on his coat and straightened his tie.

There was a knock on the door.

'Come in,' Angel called.

The door opened.

'Sir Charles Millhouse, Inspector,' the police constable announced.

'Thank you, Constable,' Angel responded.

The young constable nodded and disappeared down the corridor.

There stood a very tall, slim man.

Angel observed the jet-black wavy hair, probably dyed he thought, the tailored camel hair coat, the handmade silk shirt, the plain bright blue tie, and the pasty cheeks pushing their way through a fading Caribbean suntan, and, unexpectedly, the need of a shave.

'Come in, sir,' he said, forcing a smile. 'I'm Detective Inspector Angel. What can I do for you?'

Sir Charles approached him to shake his hand. The policeman noticed the smell of tobacco. He could have eaten a cigarette.

'Are you the man in charge, Inspector?' Sir Charles said in an accent somewhere between Eton and Oxford.

'Please take a seat, Sir Charles. I'm the most senior officer available,' he lied. 'What can I do for you?'

'I want to see the top man: the chief constable.'

'He's out. Now what can I do for you?'

'Isn't there an assistant chief constable I can see?'

'We don't have one.'

He pointed to the chair in front of his desk. They both sat down. Sir Charles grunted his displeasure, pushed a lock of shiny black hair back from his face, crossed his legs elegantly, displaying his handmade calfskin boots. Angel noticed that they were muddy not only on the soles but also the uppers. That was unexpected.

'As I tried to explain to the man on the desk — he wouldn't let me past the barrier — my wife has disappeared. I got back from the city last night — she wasn't in the house. It was very unusual. I have been phoning all the places where I thought she could have been — even the hospital. I wondered if she had been taken ill. My son has not heard from her at all this week. I have been everywhere looking for her. We have a housekeeper and a gardener. They left at four o'clock yesterday afternoon, as they always do. They said that everything was as usual. I am at a loss . . .'

His voice trailed away to nothing. He shrugged and then shook his head.

Angel said, 'You've tried her friends, family, the hospital?'

Sir Charles nodded.

'You have just the one son?'

'Yes. He's *my* son. Yvette is my second wife. He has an antique business.'

Angel nodded and moved on. 'Could she have taken it into her mind to go away for any reason? A holiday, or to visit a friend you don't even know?'

'No.'

'Have you considered that she may have left you deliberately?'

Angel could see by the twist of the man's mouth that he didn't like that question.

There was a short pause before he replied. 'Certainly not!'

'Did she leave a note?'

'No.'

'You have looked in all the likely places?'

He shook his head. 'There is no note, Inspector,' he said firmly. 'I am completely bewildered.'

There was another pause. For some reason, Angel had difficulty in raising sympathy for Charles Millhouse. Perhaps it was envy of his wealth, fame and glamour. The newspapers would have you believe he was a playboy who cared very little for anyone but himself. Perhaps he really did care about his wife.

Angel flashed his big teeth in a forced smile. 'Perhaps when you get home, sir, there she'll be — waiting for you, with some perfectly reasonable explanation of it all.'

9

'I doubt it,' he replied quietly and then he added, 'And there's something else. Very odd. It may be irrelevant. Seems ridiculous. But a hearthrug is missing.'

'A hearthrug? A carpet?'

'Yes.'

Angel pursed his lips. 'It wasn't valuable was it? A work of art?'

'No. No.'

'About what size?'

'Oh,' he began impatiently. 'About eight feet by fifteen feet, I suppose. It was in front of the hearth in the drawing room at the Hall. It had been there as long as I can remember.'

Angel pursed his lips. 'What colour?'

'I don't know. Maroon background, I think. Jacobean pattern with blue, purple and so on. It's been there for so long, I can hardly remember what it looked like.'

Angel noted the details. 'Strange. And that's all that's missing?'

Sir Charles waved the question away. 'Well, what are you going to do about finding my wife, Inspector?'

The policeman gripped the arms of his chair tightly. 'Obviously, she isn't a minor. It would be extremely serious if she was. There's no signs of violence, no note. Your wife is perfectly entitled to leave the house whenever she chooses.'

Sir Charles's lips tightened. 'Of course she's not a minor,' he roared. 'And it is still extremely serious! My wife hasn't left the house in the ordinary course of events.'

'She was at home yesterday?' Angel asked evenly.

'According to my housekeeper, she was.'

'So she has not been missing twenty-four hours yet?'

'No. She was at the house at four o'clock, yesterday afternoon. The gardener was at the house all day too. He can confirm that.'

Angel made the decision he had been trying to avoid. He had about as much work on his plate as he could manage. 'Right. I'm going to take a full description of your wife and I'll need a photograph — a recent one — and I will initiate preliminary enquiries.'

Sir Charles ran his hand over his forehead and through his hair. 'Well, I suppose that's a start.'

Angel grabbed a piece of paper out of the desk drawer. 'What's her full name?'

'Lady Yvette Millhouse.'

The policeman began writing quickly.

'Age?'

'Thirty-seven.'

Angel looked up and stared at him.

'I mean forty-one,' he said with an embarrassed, short-lived smile.

The inspector shook his head and carried on writing.

'Height, weight, hair colouring. Any special distinguishing marks?'

'Height, about five feet six inches. Weight, I don't know — but she is slim, and she's blonde with blue eyes. Inspector, she is beautiful. She is *my* wife!' he said, holding up his arms, expressively.

The inspector ignored the gesture. He was busy writing. 'That's about it for now; but I'll need that photograph. I'll call at your house this evening, if that would be convenient?'

'Anytime. The sooner the better,' he said, waving a hand for emphasis. 'You know where I live?'

'*Everybody* knows where you live, Sir Charles — I pass it every day coming here. It's the largest house in Bromersley,' he replied dryly.

The corners of the MP's mouth turned up for a second. He enjoyed the policeman's observation. He thought it was a compliment.

11

Inspector Angel stood up, opened the door and indicated to Sir Charles to lead the way. 'Try not to worry, sir. We'll do everything we can.'

'Er — thank you, Inspector.'

As Angel followed him out through the door, there was that smell of tobacco again, also a perfumed French soap. He also noticed that the MP was an inch or two taller than he was. That would make him six feet two.

Sir Charles looked vacantly first one way then the other down the olive-green corridor.

'That way. Through the double doors, past the reception desk and you're at the entrance.' The man nodded and, pulling on his tight leather driving gloves, he set off out of the building.

Angel stood with his hands in his pockets at the door of his office and watched the man walk briskly down the corridor.

A woman police constable came running up towards him panting. Her mouth open, her eyes like two fried eggs. 'Excuse me, sir. Is that Sir Charles Millhouse?'

He turned to look at her. 'Yes.'

The young woman's eyebrows shot up and her mouth opened wider. She let out a long 'wow.' And ran down the corridor to the double doors after him.

'He's old enough to be your father,' Angel called after her and then shook his head.

She didn't hear him.

'What is it women see in millionaires?' He grunted. He sauntered pensively into his office and closed the door, shaking his head.

A thought occurred to him. He leaned over the desk, quickly picked up the phone and pressed a button. He spoke urgently.

'Constable, Sir Charles Millhouse — a posh chap — camel hair coat, expensive tan, will be passing you anytime now — get the index number of the car he leaves in, also, see if he has anyone in the car with him, hurry man.'

He slammed the handset down and ran his hand thoughtfully across his mouth. He could do with something. He blew out a sigh. He knew what it was. He could murder a cigarette! He slumped down in the padded chair, opened a desk drawer and pulled out a pile of papers. He dug deeper and pulled out more letters and reports. He dumped them on the desktop. He was certain there was an opened packet of cigarettes somewhere in that desk. He got a hand to the back of the drawer when the phone rang.

'Angel,' he grunted down the handset.

It was the constable on the desk.

'Ah yes. Just a minute, lad.' He fumbled around for a pen. 'Yes. Go on.'

The constable gave him the car number and said that a young woman with blonde hair in a chauffeur's cap had driven Sir Charles away. Angel scrawled the number on the nearest piece of paper to him.

'Thanks, lad.'

He grinned as he dropped the phone back in its cradle. He tore the piece of paper with the number of the car off the bottom of a letter and looked at it. He picked up the phone and pressed a button.

'Send that new cadet into my office, pronto.'

A few seconds elapsed and there was a tap at the door.

'Come in,' Angel bawled.

It was Cadet Ahaz.

'You wanted me, sir?' Ahmed asked politely.

13

Angel handed him the scrap of paper. 'Run that through your computer and see what you come up with. Can you do that?'

'Oh yes, sir,' he replied, opening wide his big brown eyes and smiling with enthusiasm.

Angel grinned. 'Go on then. And let me know what you find — quick sharp.'

Ahmed ran out of the office, closing the door behind him. He was pleased to be doing something obviously important and useful.

The inspector continued scratching around the back of the drawer for cigarettes.

The phone rang. Angel sighed and picked up the receiver. It was Gawber.

'Yes, Ron . . . A witness? Does she? . . . Will she stand up in court? . . . Good. Any sign of a shotgun? . . . Oh. *You've got to find that gun* . . . Keep at it, Ron. Speak to you later.'

There was a knock at the door.

'Come in,' the inspector called, as he replaced the receiver.

It was Ahmed holding forth a sheet of paper.

'Details of that car you wanted, sir,' he said with a big smile. 'Was that "quick sharp" enough for you, sir?' he added confidently.

'Aye, ta,' Angel said, showing a quick smile and snatching the small, folded piece of paper. Then, flashing his teeth, he added, 'Off you go. It's time you went home to your non-smoking mother.'

Ahmed's eyes opened wide. His small, handsome square jaw stiffened. He looked straight into Angel's craggy face. 'Nobody smokes in our house, sir. It is a dirty habit and my mother is a very clean lady.'

Angel sniffed and looked at his watch. 'Well, go home and annoy her then.'

The smile left Ahmed's face. He turned smartly to the door, and with his hand on the handle added, 'I do not annoy my mother. *Goodnight, sir!*'

The door slammed shut.

Angel smiled as he glanced down at the paper and began to read the details of the licence plate of Sir Charles Millhouse's car. Then the smile left him, his jaw dropped and he screwed up his eyebrows.

...

TWO

It was seven o'clock that same evening, and already very dark in a cloudy sky.

Detective Inspector Angel drove the new, standard issue, two-litre, unmarked police car, from the front of the modern semi-detached bungalow on the new estate where he lived.

He took the country road for a mile, bypassing the centre of Bromersley, and then up the hill to Millhouse Hall. His car headlights picked out the big black iron gates, which were standing wide open, ahead of him. He went straight through the entrance, past the sign marked 'Private,' along a curved drive, between huge Canadian redwood conifers leaning inwards from each side. He then passed smaller trees and bushes until the road straightened out into a long stretch, bordered by a big expanse of cleared grass on both sides and leading up to the black painted wooden doors of the big Georgian stone house immediately ahead.

Angel drove up to the front of the house. Gravel crunched noisily and sprayed from the tyres as he swung the car round. A Silver Cloud Rolls Royce and a Citroen estate car standing in front of the house were caught in the headlights. He parked his car alongside them and noted the registration number of the foreign car on the back of an envelope from his inside pocket. He never knew when it might come in handy. He pulled on the handbrake, doused the lights and switched off the ignition. Six powerful lights mounted on the front of the house suddenly illuminated the parking area and front steps. Angel shielded his eyes as he kicked his way through the noisy gravel.

The black door opened and Sir Charles Millhouse appeared at the top of ten wide stone steps. His face, at first, seemed to indicate disappointment as he looked down at the inspector. Then he smiled.

'Oh it's you, my dear fellow. Come in,' he said to Angel unexpectedly cordially. 'Come in. Come in.'

Sir Charles was still dressed as he had been earlier at the station. He was still wearing the camel hair overcoat.

Angel noted that the man must have known of his arrival. He must have a heat responsive alarm system installed, or closed-circuit television with night vision. Not surprising for a small family living in a big house in its own extensive grounds.

'Good evening, sir,' Angel said, as he trudged up the steps into the house. He looked round at the large oak-panelled hall and wide oak staircase leading up to a balustraded balcony with four or five closed doors just visible from the front door. Downstairs in the centre of the hall was a long, highly polished table. Everything was spotless and there was the smell of recently polished furniture. He noticed the tiny red intruder alarm light blinking at him from under the balcony.

Sir Charles rushed ahead, swiftly snatching a half full tumbler of an amber coloured liquid from the long table as he passed. Then looking back he said quickly, 'Close the door, old chap. And then come on through here.'

17

He disappeared at speed passing several doors and down a long passageway.

Angel closed the big wooden front door and muttered something inaudible about, 'not being a rich man's lackey.' He followed the man down the wide passageway. It led into a kitchen of mammoth proportions with spotless white walls and a scrubbed tiled floor. In the corner was another intruder alarm light. On the table in the centre of the room were packets and tins and plates and cutlery and all manner of culinary ingredients and equipment. At the stove was the smell of a frying pan with hot fat spitting noisily into which an egg had been dropped.

Sir Charles was standing over the pan. He looked back at Angel. 'Sorry about the abrupt greeting. Have you any news?'

'No, sir. Have you?'

'No. You caught me at a critical time. I am making myself an egg sandwich. Will you join me?'

'No, ta,' Angel grunted. 'I only came for a photograph of your wife.'

He stood by the door, looking around at the walls, the floor and the powerful strip lights on the high ceiling. He took everything in, but his face maintained a disinterested expression.

'Ah yes,' Sir Charles said, flipping hot fat over the top of the egg, jumping in the pan. 'You'll have a drink?'

'No thanks.'

'Of course,' the MP said knowingly. 'On duty.'

'Got to get back. I want to get that photograph copied and in circulation.'

'Will you just give me a minute to finish this, Inspector?'

Angel looked at his wristwatch. 'I suppose so.'

The hot fat threw up blue smoke and a burning smell most of which sailed up to the huge shiny copper hood of an extractor

18

fan. The policeman rubbed his big nose and turned towards the door. He could not help wondering where the 'help' was. Why was a man in his position preparing his own meal?

'Where is everybody?'

Sir Charles slapped the egg in the bread roll and put it on a plate. 'Sure you won't have a drink, Inspector?'

'No thanks.' He replied sullenly.

'The house is empty because my wife is missing, isn't she?' He said pointedly. 'We can't get staff to live in these days. Please follow me. I'll get you that photograph.'

Sir Charles took the plate and his glass out of the kitchen and across the hall to a large room with a grand piano, two settees and ten or more easy chairs. A huge imitation gas fire was burning in the big grate. A long-cased clock with its pendulum swinging stood near the fireplace. A large oil painting of Sir Charles in army officers' uniform was hanging on the chimneybreast.

'Very nice,' Angel said surveying the room. With a nod to the portrait, he added, 'In the army were you, then?'

'Briefly, Inspector. Saw service in the Falklands. Not much fun.'

'No, sir.'

Sir Charles took a big bite out of the sandwich and then crossed over to the piano. There were twenty or so photographs in silver or wooden frames covering the top of the piano. Most of the photographs were of family groups, or of twos and some single portraits. He pointed to several of a young, pretty woman.

'Take your pick, Inspector. The beautiful woman you see there is *my wife*.'

Angel surveyed the photographs. 'Which is the latest? And which looks most like her?'

Sir Charles took another bite of the sandwich, put the plate down, picked up a framed photograph and without a word handed it to the policeman.

Angel took the photograph out of its frame and slipped it into his pocket.

'I'll see you get it back, sir.'

'Thank you.'

Angel was turning to leave when he noticed a polished silver box, highly decorated with filigree work, on the piano top in front of the photographs. He turned back. It looked as if it might contain cigarettes. His eyes hovered over the box for a brief moment. His hand ran across his mouth.

Sir Charles noticed his interest and picked the box up.

'Attractive, isn't it?'

Angel sniffed and nodded. 'Suppose so.'

'Solid silver. Bought it in America, at Tiffany's, actually,' he said, holding it in the palm of his hand. 'It's for cigarettes, of course.'

He opened the lid.

Angel's eyebrows lifted as he peered inside.

'But it's empty,' Sir Charles said a little surprised. 'Nobody in this house smokes cigarettes. I must have it refilled. It is nice to be able to offer them to guests.'

The policeman grunted.

There was a knock on the open drawing room door. He turned to see a pretty young woman with long blonde hair, and wearing a grey trouser suit with a white blouse collar sticking out of the coat.

Angel was surprised. He thought there was only the two of them in the house.

Sir Charles turned to the door. 'Yes?' he said sharply.

'Will you be wanting me anymore this evening, sir?' she said.

Angel could have sworn she gave a slight twist of the mouth that ended in a smile, and a little swing of the hips as she spoke. He was tired and bored; it could have been his imagination, or mischievous thinking, or merely nicotine withdrawal symptoms.

Sir Charles's mouth tightened. 'No. No thank you.' He snapped. 'Be here at ten o'clock in the morning. All right?' he said quickly.

She looked Angel up and down and then flashed a smile across at Sir Charles.

'Goodnight then, sir.'

'Goodnight,' Sir Charles said through his teeth.

She looked back at Inspector Angel. 'Goodnight to you, too.'

The policeman grinned. 'Goodnight, lass.'

She disappeared. A few seconds later, the big outside door slammed shut.

'That's my driver,' Sir Charles said looking into his glass. 'I don't know how she got in. I mean she *was* supposed to have gone home. She lives in the town . . . somewhere.'

Angel smiled. 'You don't have to explain to me, sir.'

Sir Charles noticed the policeman's expression. His dark eyes flashed. 'But I do,' he replied angrily.

'It's not at all necessary.'

The glass in his hand shook. 'It is. It is. I do. I do,' he spluttered, and then, more evenly he added, 'Well, anyway, I want to. I don't want any misunderstanding. I don't want you misconstruing anything. Her name is Melanie Bright. She lives with her parents in the town. Her father works in the Town Hall. Very respectable family. She's just a driver, a chauffeur . . . *nothing else.*'

'It never occurred to me that she *was* anything else,' he lied. 'I deal only in facts, sir. I don't make assumptions,' Angel said, still smiling.

Sir Charles was red in the face.

The policeman deliberately wiped his hand across his mouth.

Sir Charles's eyes shone as if they were illuminated with a light source from the back of his head. Then, after a few seconds, he smiled. 'You didn't lock the door, did you — when you came in? — I had to dash into the kitchen.'

'I didn't lock any door, sir. That's quite correct,' Angel said quietly.

Sir Charles's composure returned. 'Yes, that's what happened. She let herself in. Probably came in through the back door. Yes. The outside lights didn't come on. A buzzer sounds when the outside security lights come on, you see. It didn't buzz, did it? You didn't hear it buzz, did you, Inspector?'

'No.'

'She must have come in through the kitchen, by the *back* door. I must have opened it and left it unlocked. Don't you see? She came back. And she let herself in by the *back* door. She came back — to see if I needed to be driven anywhere. Yes, that's it. *She came back and let herself in by the back door.*'

He sighed and forced a smile. He was composed now that he had delivered that explanation.

Angel flashed his big teeth. But it was not his usual grin: that red, leathery face was hiding more than he intended to admit. His questions would wait. He was tired. He'd had enough of the day. Home was the only place he wanted to be on that cold November night. If it hadn't been for seeing the pretty smiling face of Melanie Bright, the evening would have been a total bore. And he experienced plenty of boring evenings in Bromersley, especially in the winter. He buttoned up his raincoat.

'Well, I'll be off, Sir Charles.'

'Er, yes,' the tall man said thoughtfully.

Angel turned to leave.

Suddenly, there was the sound of a buzzer coming from the hall. It lasted but two seconds. Sir Charles's eyes shone. He stood motionless in the drawing room glass in hand.

'There,' he said, as if he had made an important discovery. 'Someone is on the portico. The outside security lights switch has been triggered. All the lights will be lit.'

Angel looked across at him wondering whether he was going to open the door. 'It could be your wife, Sir Charles?'

Before he could reply, there was the clatter of the front door opening, the voice of a man calling out, followed by the bang of the heavy door being closed.

Sir Charles put his glass down on the wine table near the fireplace. He looked past Angel to the drawing room door leading from the hall. A burly, muscular man of around thirty years, strode quickly into the room, closely followed by a slim, attractive brunette wearing a tight skimpy red dress.

Sir Charles's jaw dropped. 'Oh, it's you two.'

They brushed past Inspector Angel and Sir Charles and made a straight line for the fire.

'Has Yvette turned up then?' The young man asked.

'No,' Sir Charles replied bluntly. He stared from the man to the woman and back in quick succession. Then looked across at Angel. 'My son and his wife, Duncan and Susan.'

Angel nodded. 'Ah, yes. The antique dealer?'

Duncan looked up briefly. 'Yes.' Then he looked at his father sourly.

Both Duncan Millhouse and his wife leaned towards the fire and put out their hands to warm them. Then the pretty young woman left the fire briefly and came across to Sir Charles. She stood on tiptoe and gave him a peck on the cheek.

'Hello, Pa.'

'Hello Susie,' he said quietly with a very short smile.

'Sorry about Yvette,' she said and returned to the fire.

'I expect she'll turn up,' Sir Charles said, shaking his head and then biting his lower lip. He then looked at Angel.

Duncan stopped warming his hands and turned round for a chance to warm his back and legs. He had long, thick arms filling out a dark lounge suit, was much shorter than his father, and more athletic. He glanced at the podgy policeman and said casually, as he straightened his coat collar, 'Who's this then?'

'Inspector Angel.'

'Good evening,' Angel grunted.

'Police, eh? Good evening. I hope you're going to find my stepmother soon,' he said coolly.

'We will. We will,' he replied, trying to sound confident.

'A lovely woman.'

'I'm sure she is.'

The policeman didn't take to the brashness of this young man. His voice was loud. His jaw stuck out. He moved with short, jerky actions. His father could teach him a lot about personal charm and presentation. Angel then looked across at Susan Millhouse. He observed her glistening, short, black hair and trim figure. How elegant she was in contrast to her husband. Surely, he thought, she could have found a more presentable partner.

'I'll be off, then, Sir Charles.'

He turned to the door, then turned back briefly. 'Good evening, everybody.'

'I'll see you out,' Sir Charles said. 'You *will* let me know if you hear anything.'

'You'll be the first to know, sir,' he grunted.

'Thank you, Inspector. Goodnight.'

Angel heard the door close behind him and the heavy bolt slide across. It was dark, late, and he was tired. He stood under the covered porch in the glare of the outside lights and looked out into the November mist. He shook his head in thought. What people!

He looked down at the assembly of cars standing on the gravel frontage. There was the Silver Cloud, the Citroen, a black Mercedes and his own car. So which car had Sir Charles's driver gone home in? It wasn't the Citroen. That was still there. Duncan Millhouse presumably owned the Mercedes. Inspector Angel rubbed his hand across his mouth. Would the glamorous chauffeur still be around with Sir Charles's son and daughter-in-law in the house? She might. A bit risky? Maybe she walked home? It was a long way on foot to anywhere from here.

Without thinking, he slapped the pockets of his coat feeling for a packet of cigarettes. When he realized what he was doing, he stopped. He knew he hadn't any. It was another of those habits he would have to break. But there were times when a man needed a cigarette, he reckoned — and this was one of them.

It was not easy being a policeman: you start looking for a crime and then for a suspect! After twenty years on the job sometimes you find a suspect first and then start looking for a crime! But this was *simply a case of a missing person*; and she's only been missing about thirty hours. There are *hundreds* of missing persons. Why is a detective inspector involving himself in a run of the mill enquiry like this? There was a detective sergeant, Ron Gawber, chasing after an armed robber, and he, Angel, a detective inspector, involving himself in what might finish up being simply a case of a runaway wife! The chief constable might have him over the coals if he knew what he was doing. Wasting time, he would have said, and *delegate, delegate, delegate*, he would have yelled.

Angel was about to pick his way down the stone steps, when he heard the angry, muffled voice of a man through the stout door behind him. He moved round behind the nearest pillar as the door rattled open.

It was Duncan Millhouse.

'You can't talk to me like that anymore,' he was shouting.

Sir Charles Millhouse replied in a restrained voice. 'Come back in, you fool. That policeman may be still around.'

Duncan replied quietly. 'I don't care. I'm going. Come on, Susan.'

'Don't be stupid. This is a time for us to stick together. Talk to him Susie. Talk some sense into him.'

'I don't care,' Duncan Millhouse replied, more calmly.

'Come back in, for God's sake. Let's talk about this like adults.'

There was a short silent pause, then the door slammed and peace reigned once more.

Angel stepped forward into the light. There was a smile on his face. He got into his car and drove out of the tall iron gates on to the main road. The low mist required him to weave slowly along the country road. It was a direct straight way to the station now. He peered through the screen wipers as they swept across the rain spots. He wondered why a big cheese like Sir Charles Millhouse MP himself stopped and called in the police station, when he would know that a telephone call to the station would have had Bromersley Police rushing over to his mansion to do a bit of bowing and scraping. Millhouse was an educated man, not an academic, but an MP. He was an image maker. A maker of public opinion. A mind changer. A mind bender. A maker of spin. Spin? Yes. He puts a slant on events to make them seem different to what they really are. Yes. But all MPs do that. That's their job. But that about sums him up.

His son, Duncan, was a very different character. He had the charm of a fridge. No manners. Perhaps a bit of a bully. Probably be good at breaking his friends' toys. A good rugby prop forward. A weightlifter. An athletic lump. He had no charm though. He wouldn't favourably impress Daddy's friends, would he? Angel grinned. And how would he make out with the girls? Of course, Daddy's money would be a big attraction. Or even Daddy himself. Marrying the son would put a woman nearer the father, and nearer the money. *That* might be important. Susan Millhouse *was* a bit of a bobby dazzler. She *was* lovely to look at, and she carried herself well. She had given Daddy-in-law a dutiful peck on the cheek. He wondered what her background was. She wasn't your common or garden tart. Angel pulled himself up short. He had seen very little of her. He should reserve judgment. Her presence in the family probably didn't matter a hoot. She was probably only there to 'dress the set.'

The more serious matter was the missing Lady Yvette Millhouse. He had only the physical description of her. He knew nothing of her personality, her likes and dislikes, or the causes, reasons and explanations for her disappearance. Finding her was going to be tough, he reflected. There's nothing to go on. No obvious discord, no rows, no obvious hatred, jealousies or third parties. Not yet anyway. *Give it time*, he mused. Give it time.

* * *

It was eight twenty-five the next morning. There was no sun. It was still gloomy that November day as Inspector Angel drove his car past the blue illuminated sign bearing the words 'police station' yet again. The area at the rear was still illuminated by powerful halogen lights, casting a yellow shadow on the half dozen or so parked cars in the yard.

He parked up and went through the glass door into the station.

The constable at the desk saw him wave, nodded, and pushed the release button to allow him through the security door. He peered into the CID office. The glaring strip lights suspended from the ceiling were all on, but there was no one there. He looked up at the clock. It was eight-thirty exactly. He grunted loudly, switched off the lights, closed the door and made his way to his own office. He flopped into the chair behind his desk and picked up the phone. He pressed the button for the reception desk.

'Constable, do you happen to have any cigarettes out there?'

'Sorry, sir. I don't smoke.'

'Right, lad,' he replied with a loud sigh. 'Hmmm. Where is everybody?'

'They're out on traffic, sir, some of them anyway. There's been a big pile up on the M1. The late shift *and* the early shift are out there.'

'Right, lad. Thank you.'

He returned the phone to its cradle and dug into his inside pocket and pulled out his wallet containing the photograph of the missing woman. He switched on his desk lamp and looked at it carefully. It was a studio posed photograph of postcard size, showing a beautiful smiling woman, aged about thirty-five, with short blonde permed hair and wearing an off the shoulder dress, sitting with her hands delicately positioned one upon the other on the lap. She was also wearing long earrings with prominent green stones in them and encrusted with what appeared to be diamonds; she wore a ring on the third finger of her left hand which had a large green stone in the centre of it, also surrounded by what appeared to be diamonds. On the back was the rubber stamp of the name, 'Marcus La Touche.'

'Foreign,' Angel said aloud. 'Probably French?'

There was a knock on his door.

'Yes?' he called without looking up.

It was Cadet Ahmed Ahaz.

'Good morning, sir,' he said brightly. 'I am sorry—'

'What time do you call this?'

'I was about to explain, sir. I am sorry I am late, but the buses are all over the place with the timetabling. They are exceedingly late because of the fog.'

'Oh yes,' he replied still looking down at the photograph. 'You haven't mentioned the big pile up on the M1.'

Ahmed nodded. 'I was about to mention that to you as well, sir.'

'I know you were. You should have left home earlier,' Angel growled.

'I did, sir, but—'

'Never mind. Don't do it again.'

Ahmed's jaw dropped. His big eyes opened wide. 'Don't do what again, sir?'

'Don't be late again!'

The cadet's jaw tightened. 'I can't help it, sir, if the buses do not run on time; nor can I stop accidents from happening on the roads.'

'No, you can't. Fetch me a cup of tea,' he said abruptly.

Ahmed closed the door sharply without a word.

Angel looked up and grinned, then he dropped the photograph of the beautiful Lady Yvette Millhouse wearing the extravagant jewellery on the desk in front of him. He leaned back in his chair, stretched his arms above his head and closed his eyes. He stayed in that position for a few seconds, then, suddenly, lowered his arms and dived into a drawer in his desk and pulled out a telephone directory. He bounced it loudly on the desktop in front of him and flicked open the business section to 'Antique Dealers.' There was only one in Bromersley. He dialled out the number.

'Hello. Is that the antique dealers?' he enquired deliberately vaguely.

'Yes. Bromersley Antiques. How can I help you?' a man with an oily voice enquired.

Inspector Angel spoke deliberately severely. 'I've a complaint to make. Is that Mr Millhouse speaking?'

'Oh no, sir. There's no Mr Millhouse here,' the man replied attentively.

'Oh,' Angel said, not a bit surprised, but trying to sound taken aback and angry. 'I must get in touch with Duncan Millhouse straightaway. It's about those things he sold me,' he lied.

There was a short pause. The owner of the oily voice was thinking. Eventually the man said, 'I can tell you where there is a Mr Millhouse in the business, though.' The antiques dealer was delighted to pass trouble on to a competitor. 'It *may* be the gentleman you're looking for,' he added craftily.

'Oh yes,' replied the policeman, knowing full well it *would* be the man he was seeking.

'Yes. There's a Duncan Millhouse at Northern Antiques in Leeds.'

'Northern Antiques in Leeds.' Angel smiled broadly. 'Thank you very much.'

'It's on North Main Street. A big, mock Elizabethan building opposite a petrol station. You can't miss it.'

Still smiling, he replaced the telephone. There was a tap on the door.

'Come in.'

It was Ahmed with the tea.

'Put it down there, lad,' he said pointing to a coaster he swiftly pulled out of a drawer. Ahmed turned to go.

'Have you seen DS Gawber?' Inspector Angel said as he picked up the plastic cup, took a sip of the hot tea and leaned back in his chair.

'No, sir,' Ahmed said quietly.

'He's harder to find than a thre' penny bit in a Scottish Christmas pudding.'

The telephone rang. Angel smiled.

'This'll be him.'

Ahmed turned to go. The inspector signalled him to wait. He picked up the receiver. 'DI Angel.'

It was the chief constable. The smile left his face. 'Yes, sir,' Angel replied urgently . . . 'Yes, sir.'

His voice changed. He spoke in a steely quiet tone and stood up.

'Western Beck? Yes, I know it, sir . . . What about Scenes of Crime, sir? . . . Is it male or female? . . . Right, sir.'

Ahmed felt his pulse beat faster and louder.

The inspector nodded. 'Yes, sir.' He quickly put the receiver down. Without a word, he picked up his raincoat and stuffed an arm into a sleeve as he reached out for his hat.

Cadet Ahmed Ahaz stared at him with his mouth partly open. 'What is it, sir? Is it a murder?'

Angel looked him straight in the face. He recalled the horror he had experienced on his first murder case as a young constable twenty years back. He put his hand on the young man's lean shoulder and spoke to him deliberately and softly.

'Ahmed, we don't know. I want you to find DS Gawber for me. Tell him to meet me at Western Beck.'

'Yes, sir,' the young man replied quietly.

The inspector then returned to buttoning up his coat as he bustled towards the door. 'Tell him, I don't know any details; a dead body has turned up there.'

Ahmed felt a cold, tingling sensation all the way down his spine.

THREE

Twenty minutes later, Inspector Angel arrived at Western Beck: the black, cold reservoir a few miles out of Bromersley. Fog shrouded the hills surrounding the water. Spots of icy rain dropped from the dark sky. On the bank, irregularly parked was an array of police vehicles, some with blue lights flashing. There was the Scenes of Crime plain black van, a black van from the mortuary, another two larger vans from Leeds Police Sub Aqua Squad, the surgeon's car, and DS Gawber's car.

Blue and white 'Do Not Cross' tape was entwined around the police cars and anchored on stakes in the reservoir bank. They flapped noisily in the breeze. A man in diving gear was standing on the bank talking to DS Gawber.

DI Angel slammed shut his car door against the wind, turned up his coat collar and picked his way along the soggy bank. He took one hand out of his pocket briefly to lift the tape to reach Ron Gawber.

'What you got then?'

Ron Gawber turned away from the diver, who promptly progressed to the bank and took a short jump into the weeds on the edge of the water.

'Oh. Hello, sir.'

'Well, what have you got?' Angel said irritably, sheltering his eyes from the wind and rain.

'Looks like a young woman.'

'Can't you tell?'

Gawber paused. 'Naked.'

'Well that should make it easier then, shouldn't it?'

'That's about all I know, sir. The doc's seeing to her. I haven't been here long myself.'

'Where is she?'

'In the back of the mortuary van.'

With the nod of his head, Angel indicated that that was where he was headed. Detective Sergeant Gawber followed. The police surgeon carrying a bag, and another man came out of the back door of the black van as the DI reached them.

The white-haired pathologist looked up at Angel as he pulled down his hat as a protection against the wind. He spoke in a broad Glaswegian accent you could cut with a claymore. 'It's you, Mick?'

Angel nodded. 'Who were you expecting? Elvis Presley?'

Doctor Mac shook his head. 'I thought you'd be chief constable by now.'

'If there was any justice in this world, I would be. But when I have to depend on duff information from doddery old pathologists who ought to have been put out to grass years ago, I just can't get the convictions I ought to get.' He looked round to Ron Gawber. 'Do you know, sergeant, he's so old that when he's ill, they don't send for a doctor, they send for an archaeologist!'

DS Gawber smiled.

The surgeon didn't smile. He shook his head. 'Still as cocky as ever.' He turned away from the cold wind, turned up his coat collar and made for his car. 'What's the matter, laddie? Haven't your Prozac kicked in yet?'

'Come on, Mac. You're slower now than when it's your round in The Feathers. Give.'

The white-haired man's mouth tightened. He stopped walking and pulled out a small notebook from his raincoat pocket. The information was delivered in a cold, husky, Glaswegian accent. 'Female between the ages of thirty and fifty. Naked. Blonde. Blue eyes. About five feet four. Contusions on her neck. No other obvious signs of violence.'

The doctor closed the notebook and put it back in his inside pocket.

Angel made a slight gesture in the air with a hand. 'Is that it?'

The surgeon nodded. 'For now.' He turned to make for his car.

Angel followed. 'Cause of death?'

'Don't know.'

'Any birthmarks, tattoos, operation scars, distinguishing features?'

'Not as far as I could see.'

'Needle-marks?'

'Not as far as I could see.'

'How long had she been in the water?'

'Nae long.'

'A week?'

'Maybe.'

'Any bright ideas?'

'No.'

'Right, Mac. Thanks.' Angel said thoughtfully. 'You're as much use as a bacon slicer in a synagogue,' he muttered as he walked away. He turned back and added, 'I'll ring you later.'

The police surgeon had reached his car. 'Do that,' he replied. 'Look after yourself, Mick.' He eagerly clambered in out of the cold and put his bag on the seat beside him.

'You make more promises than a tart in a jeweller's shop,' Angel muttered after him.

'Mick,' the pathologist called mischievously as he closed the car door and wound down the window.

Angel leaned eagerly into the car window. 'What?'

'I think you're putting on weight.'

'And you should lay off the booze, because that Zimmer frame's closer than you think!' Angel retaliated as he turned away to DS Gawber.

The surgeon called out again. 'Oh, Mick!' The policeman turned back to the Scotsman's car. 'Now what?'

'Mick. There is one thing,' he said, without a smile.

The detective licked his lips expectantly and put his ear close to the car window.

'What is it?'

The elderly doctor said quietly, 'You wouldn't happen to have a cigarette on you, would you?'

* * *

'Sit down,' Angel said to Ron Gawber indicating the chair at the other side of his desk. 'I'm knackered. And these cases are building up quicker than the queue at the crematorium.'

He slumped in his chair and lifted up the phone. 'Ahmed, come in here and bring three teas with you, pronto.'

He slammed the phone down. 'My mouth's drier than a camel's powder puff.'

He looked attentively across at Ron Gawber. 'You'd better bring me up to date on this off-licence case. I can't do anything about this Millhouse job until I hear from Mac the Knife. There's nothing *more* pressing, is there?'

'I don't think we have a case, if I can't get Harry Hull to confess. And I don't think we've any chance of that.' Ron Gawber sighed. 'I'm worn out with it, sir. I think we're on a loser.'

'Harry Hull? Harry Hull? Don't I know him?' Angel said, rubbing his chin. 'A name like that stays with you.'

'He's been down before. Nothing to do with firearms, though. Housebreaking. Receiving. A couple of motoring offences. A factory break in. Harry Hull comes from Manchester. A big, ugly brute. Six-foot. A jaw like a gorilla. His mother died in mysterious circumstances. He was accused of suffocating her and then trying to stuff her into a breadbin. Stupid jury let him off.'

'Yes,' Angel said, suddenly raising his eyebrows. 'I remember. It was known as the "Mother's Pride" case. I know him. I know Harry Hull. Of course, I know him! He was a mate of Barry Scudamore, and Scott and Scrap Scudamore,' Angel said leaning back in his chair. 'Married to Ingrid Hull. Great friend of Edie Scudamore. Yes. I know Harry Hull. He's as much use as an ice cream sundial. Go on then, tell me about it.'

'Well, two men went into that Pakistani off-licence on the Bradford Road at eight o'clock on a Friday night last October. One of them — Harry Hull, we think — was carrying a sawn-off shotgun wrapped in a plastic bag. The other had a baseball bat.'

'Oh yes.'

'They were both wearing scarves or balaclavas. They threatened the owner — Injar Patel — a man in his sixties. The usual. Empty the till or else. There's only Patel in the shop at the time. A scuffle follows. The old man tried to take

37

the gun off Hull and in the scuffle Hull hits him on the head with it. Then his wife comes in from the back room behind them, sees what's happening, she screams, they both turn nasty. Patel is on the floor. Hull's accomplice makes to belt Mrs Patel with the bat. Patel gets up off the floor, opens the till, gives them all the money there is . . . about a hundred quid, he says . . . and they run off. Later, Mrs Patel picks out Harry Hull from our pix, although she could only see half his face. His height, his eyes, his ears, his skin, as well as the rest of his clothes — his imitation leather jacket, jeans and trainers, all fit her description. Hull's alibi was that he was with his wife, Ingrid, all that evening, watching the telly. Of course, she confirms it. We have no trace of the other man — the one with the baseball bat.'

Ron Gawber leaned back in his chair.

'And how badly was the old man hurt?'

'A bit early to say. Two stitches in his head. He seems all right. His wife was badly shook up. On pills for depression now. Nice people. It's only a little tin pot business, you know. I don't know how they scratch a living out of it.'

Angel nodded.

There was a knock on the door.

'Come in.'

It was Cadet Ahmed Ahaz with a small tray of plastic teacups.

Angel looked up. 'We're surrounded by Indians.'

Ahmed glared at him.

'Put them down there, lad. And take a pew.'

'What is this about being "surrounded by Indians," sir?' Ahmed asked coldly.

Angel sighed again, but louder. 'Just a joke, boy. Nothing more.'

'Oh, I see, sir,' he replied, his jaw fixed. 'Not a very funny joke, sir. Nobody is laughing.'

Angel shook his head. 'Don't be so touchy, lad. DS Gawber and I have just been talking about this Patel case, and—'

'Mr Patel is *not* an Indian. He is from Pakistan,' Ahmed said, brusquely.

'Is he? All right then. Now can we get on? Just sit there and listen. See what you can learn.'

Ahmed picked up his tea and sat down in a chair by the wall.

Angel swivelled back in his chair to the DS. 'So, what it amounts to is that we need to break Hull's alibi.'

'Yes, sir. That's it. But his wife is a hard nut too, sir. Her name is Ingrid. I've interviewed her. Streetwise, you might say. *She'll not give him away.*'

Angel nodded quickly. 'We've met.'

'We can only hold him until eight o'clock in the morning. Unless we can get another warrant, which I doubt.'

'Harry Hull. Harry Hull,' Angel muttered as he dropped his chin on to his chest and shook his head. 'I must be getting old. There's something about him. I just can't dredge it up. I can't remember like I used to.'

After a few seconds of silence, he looked up. 'Where's Barry Scudamore, these days?'

'He couldn't have been the accomplice, sir. He's in Durham doing time.'

Angel suddenly smiled. 'Of course, Barry Scudamore. Red hair!'

'You remember now, sir?'

'Of course. You can't be a villain and have red hair. It's against all the laws of commonsense. But then, he's thicker than a politician's Filofax.'

Ahmed looked across engrossed. 'Sir, can I ask a question?'

Angel looked back at the young man. 'What is it, lad?'

'Why cannot a villain have red hair?'

'Well, he can. But red hair makes him too conspicuous in a crowd or a line up.'

Ahmed nodded his understanding.

Angel continued. 'Sticks out like a monkey's bum. Yes. Come across him a few times. Well, well, well. Hasn't he learned *that* yet?' Suddenly his eyes brightened. He muttered something and then said, 'Yes, Edie Scudamore! Edie Scudamore! I remember.' He jumped up from the desk. 'Well, well, well. I think we might nail this Harry Hull, Ron.'

DS Gawber's jaw dropped open.

'What cell is he in?'

'Number two, sir.'

'Hang on here. I'll just nip down and have a look. Make sure.'

Angel bounced out of the office, down the green corridor to the custody suite. He had a word with a constable who unlocked the door and he crept on tiptoe to a cell and peered through the observation grille.

There was a big, middle-aged man with black hair, in jeans, a shirt and trainers, lounging on a bench-bed reading a newspaper.

Angel slowly smiled. He silently closed the observation grille and returned to his office.

'That's my boy,' he said rubbing his hands.

Ron Gawber smiled without knowing the reason.

Angel's smile suddenly left him. 'Ron, there are two things I must be certain of.'

'Yes, sir?'

'I must be certain that Scudamore is still locked up, and that his wife is still the same one — Edie.'

Ron rose to his feet. 'Well, I can soon check on the whereabouts of Barry Scudamore, sir.'

'Use the phone in CID, Ron.'

'It will only take a minute.'

He went out of the office.

Angel dragged the phone book out of his office drawer. There weren't many Scudamores in the book. In fact, just the one, 'B. Scudamore.'

The inspector dialled the number.

It rang out.

Brrr. Brrr.

It kept on ringing out. Angel's mouth turned down at the corners and his eyes closed. He drummed his fingers on the desktop.

Suddenly there was a click followed by a woman's voice.

'Hello. Who's that?' It was a loud cry like a cockatoo.

Angel brightened up. 'Hello. How are you, Edie?' he said in a warm, friendly voice.

'Who's that?' she squawked back.

'It *is* Mrs Edie Scudamore, isn't it?'

'No. It's the Queen of bloody Sheba. Who is it? Who is it? Who the hell is it?'

Angel smiling, gently replaced the receiver.

Ron Gawber came in. 'That's all right, sir. Barry Scudamore is safely tucked up in Durham jail and is likely to be until next July at the earliest.'

'That's great, Ron! That's great! We'll bottle this today, with a bit of luck,' Angel said beaming, then he turned to Ahmed. 'Have you ever done any acting, lad?'

Ahmed rose to his feet. 'Oh no, sir.'

'Then you are about to become a contender for an Oscar!'

'I want to be a copper, not an actor!' said Ahmed.

41

Angel ignored his pleas turned to Ron Gawber and said, 'Here's what we do.'

* * *

At three o'clock, an hour later, Detective Inspector Angel and Cadet Ahmed Ahaz walked through the custody suite door to cell number two, accompanied by the duty constable.

Ahmed was no longer in his usual smart dark suit, white shirt and dark tie, but in a sloppy pair of jeans, pullover, trainers and baseball cap.

Angel held him by the forearms and silently positioned him with his back to the corridor wall out of vision outside the cell door. He looked him straight in the face, gave him a wink and whispered, 'You'll be all right. Do exactly what I told you.'

Ahmed stood there, breathing deeply, looking at the ceiling and fidgeting with his fingers.

Angel looked at the duty constable and put up his thumb to show he was ready.

The constable looked through the grill, rattled his keys, stuck one in the lock and opened up the cell door.

'Hull, you've a visitor,' he said, leaving the cell door wide open. Then, expertly swinging the keys and chain, he ambled down the short corridor and noisily locked the suite door.

DI Angel appeared in the open cell doorway, his face expressionless. He stood there, square on, his arms down by his sides, feet slightly apart. He stared across the cell at the prisoner.

Harry Hull put down the newspaper he had been reading and got up from the bed. He looked the inspector up and down with his cold, watery eyes. Then, sticking out his lantern jaw, he walked pointlessly across the tiny cell and then back again deliberately avoiding looking the policeman in the eye.

Inspector Angel maintained his position in the doorway.

Hull sat down on his bed. He stared down at the brown tiled floor. After a moment or two, he picked up the newspaper and pretended to read it.

Angel didn't move.

A few seconds passed.

Then without looking up from the paper, Hull spat out the words, 'Well, what do you want, Angel? I ain't talking.'

The policeman took a step forward into the cell. He spoke firmly. 'That's all right. There's no need for you to say anything, Harry. I'll do all the talking. You can do all the listening.' Then he added, 'For a change.'

'If this is a cross-examination, my solicitor should be present, and we should be in the interview room with the recording machine going,' he snarled.

Hull reached over to the table at the side of the bunk. There was an open packet of cigarettes, a box of matches and an ashtray. He picked out a cigarette, lit it and turned to the inspector.

Suddenly, Hull's attitude changed. 'Didn't you bring me any fags?' He asked with a sly grin.

'No,' Angel replied tightly, but he wished he had one of Hull's cigarettes between his lips at that very moment. He continued, 'This is not a cross-examination. In fact, you needn't say a word.'

The man threw the newspaper on the cell floor, leaned back full length on the bunkbed, raised his thick, tattooed arms behind his head and stared at the policeman. He took a deep, noisy suck at the cigarette. 'Well, what do you want, then?' And then he added quickly, 'I ain't answering no

43

questions. I didn't do it. I wasn't there. I don't know nuthin' about it. I'm not sayin' nuthin'.'

Angel smiled. 'I have just said — you don't have to say a thing. Just listen.' He dragged a chair from the corner of the cell and placed it about a yard from the bunkbed. He sat on it horse-back style and leaned forward, his elbows resting on the back.

He took his time starting, and when he did, he spoke quietly in a pseudo friendly conversational manner.

'Well, Harry, I was thinking the other day about this and that and the other, and I got to thinking about you and the old days. The fun we used to have. You batting old ladies about, and me batting you about. And that led me on to thinking about our mutual friend — Barry Scudamore. Red hair. Remember him? I'm sure you do. Barry and Harry. What a pair! You two were inseparable. Barry and Harry. The Bromersley duo. With names like that, you could have made hit records. And with Barry's two brothers: Scott and Scrap Scudamore, you made a brilliant quartet. A bit like the Marx Brothers. Except that you are all stupid. Thicker than Strangeways custard. Remember the Scudamores? Of course you do. Did quite a few jobs together, didn't you. That factory job. That car scam. A few housebreaking jobs. Do you remember terrorising that woman in the petrol station for a few quid. Two hundred and eighty quid, think it was. Yes, that was a laugh, wasn't it? She was seven months gone. Do you know she lost the baby she was carrying? Yes, she did. And they dragged her out of the River Don a month after that. Her husband went do-lally and is in a mental home in Huddersfield. The two kids are living on social security with their grandmother. All that for two hundred and eighty quid. But you wouldn't worry about that, would you, Harry? You wouldn't even care.

44

Anyway, that's life, isn't it? It's the way things go, isn't it, Harry? It's the way that toast falls on the carpet. Butter side down. The luck of the draw. Wasn't your fault, was it Harry? A bit like three weeks ago. Belting the living daylights out of an old Paki, for the hundred quid in his till. It's all in a day's play, isn't it, Harry? If Mrs Patel dies of a heart attack, it wouldn't be your fault, would it? As long as you and Barry and Scott and Scrap, could sink a few pints together in The Feathers, and have a few laughs with the girls in the "Can Can Club," that's all that mattered, then, wasn't it, Harry?'

Without taking his eyes off him, he paused for a second and then adopted a more serious tone.

'Do you know where Barry is these days, Harry? He's on his holidays. Gone away to get a suntan. Yes. He's in Durham. Sunny Durham. Durham Prison.'

Angel paused again. He looked closely at Harry Hull and waited. There was no reaction. He went on.

'But, of course, you know that, don't you, Harry? You know all about it. You know exactly where Barry Scudamore is. *Seeing as how you helped put him there.*'

Hull returned the stare but without any expression.

The policeman continued. 'How's his wife getting along, Harry? What's her name, Harry? What's her name? I'm not good at names.' He paused and looked at the ceiling.

'Now whatever is it?' He snapped his fingers and smiled. 'I've got it. I remember it now. Yes. It's Edie, that's her name, isn't it Harry? Edie Scudamore. Yes. The beautiful Edie.'

Harry Hull stared at him without blinking.

Angel dropped the smile. 'A right trollop if ever I saw one. They don't come much cheaper than Edie Scudamore, do they? And any man would do. Her head has bobbed up and down more times than Lady Chatterley. But she stood by Barry. When he was out of prison, that is. I'll give her that. And he's been in and out of jail more times than David Beckham has credit cards. But yes. She's stuck to him. Like the rent man on pay day. God knows why, Harry. I suppose it's because you go well together, like Abbott and Costello, Laurel and Hardy, Morecambe and Wise, and Barry and Harry.'

Angel could see Hull's face very gradually getting redder and the corners of his mouth turning downwards; but the policeman chose to disregard the changes.

'But of course, you knew Barry Scudamore's wife's name, didn't you?'

Hull remained silent.

Angel went on. 'You did, Harry. Didn't you? And I'll tell you why. Because Edie Scudamore is your sister, isn't she, Harry? She's your sister! She's *your sister*!'

Harry Hull could keep quiet no longer.

'So what!' he yelled. 'So what! What are you going on about? It's no secret! Of course she's my sister. Everybody knows she's my sister! The whole world knows she's my sister!' He waved his arms above his head. 'Some copper you are. Think you're smart, do you? Who the 'ell do you think you are? Sherlock Holmes?'

Angel sat there unmoved. He spoke even more quietly than before. 'I *know* it's no secret, Harry. Everybody who knows you in Bromersley knows that that tart, Edie Scudamore, is your sister. It's no secret. Dammit, you and her and Barry and Scott and "Scrap" have been in the papers often enough for some villainy or other for years.'

Hull opened his huge mouth like a lion. 'Aah!' he snarled.

Angel leaned forward and stared into his watery eyes. 'No that's not the secret, Harry. That's not the secret. I'm coming to that.'

Hull stubbed out the consumed cigarette and lit another quickly.

Angel started a different tack. 'I don't suppose you remember clocking a ten-year-old BMW that had done a million miles, back to about twenty thousand, do you?'

Hull stared hard at the policeman.

'That was a little job you did on your own. Barry and Scott and Scrap didn't know anything about that, did they, Harry? The evidence was a bit hazy. The fingerprints were smudged. We couldn't quite prove it. Our witness was a bit dithery. There was room for doubt. I'll give you that. But do you remember?'

The man didn't react. The policeman continued.

'Is your memory improving, Harry? Do *you* need a holiday? Maidstone's nice at this time of year. A bit of rock cake breaking? Or Wandsworth? They say it's nice in Wandsworth these days. You get your own ping-pong ball, tea pot and bucket. The head warden comes round every day at eleven o'clock with chocolate digestives. Are you looking forward to a holiday, Harry?'

Angel was getting into his stride. He added firmly, '*Because you're going to get one.* It was exactly the same time that you tipped me the wink about poor Barry and his wagonload of hot cigarettes.'

Harry Hull yelled across the cell. 'I didn't squeal. I never squeal. I didn't do a deal with you! I would never do a deal with a copper. Never!'

'Oh, you're hearing me, Harry? I'm getting through to you,' Angel continued. 'And you're remembering. That's good, Harry. Well, we didn't *call* it a deal. Coppers don't do deals with scum like you; but that's what it amounted to. A nod's as good as a wink to a blind horse, isn't it, Harry?

You told me about Barry and his cigarettes and I dropped the charge against you for clocking the BMW. It was as simple as that.'

'I never said a word to you about Barry's job!' he yelled, then turned away and looked outside through the cell bars.

Angel took a breather. 'I reckon you got a bargain. Is it all coming back to you Harry? Is it?'

He went in for the 'kill'.

'Now all it would take is a word from me to your sister, Edie. She would tell her loving husband, Barry. It would simply ruin his holiday in Durham. His stitching would go to pot. The Post Office would be losing letters all down the M1! And he would set those lovely brothers of his on to you — Scott and Scrap — and they would come looking for you. And puff! You wouldn't know whether it was Shrove Tuesday or Sheffield Wednesday. They'd cut you up into little pieces and sell you for dogmeat on Barnsley Market. I wouldn't give a tanner for your chances. And Edie wouldn't be able to keep it from Ingrid, her best friend, your wife, either, would she? Your loving, ever faithful wife, Ingrid. Oh no. Because Edie's got a mouth bigger than a tallyman's satchel. A right pair of slags together they make. And Ingrid would be off like a shot with that Italian she fancies—'

Harry Hull leaped rapidly off the bunk and put his scarlet, sweaty face six inches away from DI Angel. 'I don't have to take this!' he roared. His eyes bulging. 'I want my solicitor. You've no right to make threats. You can't interview me without it being recorded.'

He could hear his heavy breathing as he stormed past the policeman, round the back of him and then back again.

Ahmed, still waiting in the corridor, was afraid he might come out of the cell and see him secretly waiting.

Angel was surprised at the unexpected commotion, but he didn't move a muscle. He didn't even turn round when the man was behind him. 'This isn't an interview. I wasn't interviewing you, Harry. And I certainly wasn't making any threats. You've got it the wrong way round, Harry. I'm the policeman: *you're* the crook. It's *you* that does the threatening, Harry. No. Look on it as a sort of a history lesson. A blast from the past. A reminder of happier days.'

Hull wasn't listening. His big eyes moved from side to side. He passed a hand quickly through his oily hair. His heavy breathing grew faster. 'What Italian?' He suddenly yelled. 'What Italian? Who is it? Who is it?'

'I don't know, Harry. It's just what I hear,' Angel lied.

Hull wiped his sweating face with his hands and slumped down on the bunk. His closed eyes concealed his confusion.

Angel stood up and put the chair back against the wall. Then he said, 'Oh, before I go, I'd like to introduce you to a young man. You may have seen him the night you assaulted his grandfather.'

Angel stuck his neck out of the cell doorway, where Ahmed was still patiently waiting in his baggy clothes and baseball cap. 'Come in, Mr Patel,' he said to the young cadet.

Ahmed, as instructed, walked boldly into the cell. Angel pointed to Hull and said, 'Is that the man?' Ahmed looked closely at the man before he replied robustly. 'That's the man, sir.'

'Right, Mr Patel. Thank you. Please leave us. Knock on the door at the end and the constable will let you out.' Ahmed nodded and left the cell.

Angel was pleased with the young man's performance.

Harry Hull was crestfallen. 'You can't do that,' he protested. 'That's not a line up. That won't stand up in court.'

'It doesn't have to. It was exclusively for my benefit. I just needed confirmation that I wasn't going to do you an injustice, Harry,' he lied, and then he added with a broad smile, 'You know me, Harry — always want to be fair.'

'Are you saying that lad was in the Paki's shop?'

Angel nodded.

'Where was he? I never saw him. Where was he? Was he behind the Paki woman?' he stormed.

'He saw the whole thing,' Angel lied.

Harry Hull walked around the cell — as much as space allowed — shaking his head.

'Who told you it was me what done it?'

'Can't tell you that, Harry. Maybe it was one of Barry Scudamore's brothers. Maybe it was somebody else. "Information received" we call it in the trade, Harry. You know that.' The policeman made an educated guess. 'Remember poor Barry who was caught with the wagonload of cigarettes, Harry? Perhaps it was pay-off time?' Angel added slyly.

Harry Hull went scarlet. He walked around the cell with his arms in the air. 'I'll kill that Scott! I'll kill him! He never could keep his trap shut!'

Angel noted that free piece of information with great satisfaction. He didn't react. He hovered a few seconds by the door for Hull to regain his composure.

'Well, what's it to be, Harry? I haven't got all day.'

Hull slumped back on the bed. He held his head in his hands. Then he banged on the end of the bed with his hands. 'I need time.'

'You've had enough time,' Angel yelled. 'And so has Barry Scudamore!' he added pointedly.

'I want to see Blomfield. I ought to see my solicitor.' He muttered.

Angel spoke quietly. 'It's got nothing to do with law, Harry. The best barrister in the land can't sort this one out for you. It's much easier than that. It's simply a question of whether you want to live or die. Whether you want the Scudamore family, including your wife, after your blood or whether you want to stay alive. And I'd have thought the answer to that would have been easy. Still . . .' The inspector paused a second, then turned to leave. If Hull didn't break now, he never would. Angel reached the door.

'Mr Angel,' Hull called in a small voice.

The policeman turned back. 'Yes, Harry?'

'How long do you think I'll get?' He asked quietly.

FOUR

Detective Inspector Angel mopped his forehead with a handkerchief as he made his way along the green corridor to the CID room. He peered through the doorway, spotted that Ahmed was still wearing the scruffy jumper, jeans and trainers, and said, 'you'd better get out of that camouflage, lad. You look as if you've been to a blind man's jumble sale.'

Then he became aware that the seven or eight occupants of the office were staring at him and all smiling broadly.

Angel glowered back at them. 'What are you all grinning at?' He looked down at the front of his trousers. 'Is my fly undone?'

Ahmed flashed a smile and said, 'I told everybody how you stuck up for the Patels, and that you told Hull exactly what he was.'

'Yes. Er — well, you had no right to. That's confidential. Er — everybody get on with your work,' he stammered. 'This isn't Blackpool Pleasure Beach!' Then he turned back to Ahmed, 'Where's DS Gawber?'

'I don't know, sir.'

'Well, *find* him, lad. *Find* him! And send him to my office, pronto.' He turned away and then back. He glanced at Ahmed again and said, 'And *do* get out of those scruffy clothes!'

'Yes, sir. But I will have to go home.'

Angel made his way determinedly to his office.

Ahmed followed, calling after him, down the corridor. 'Sir. Please, sir.'

Angel didn't stop until he was sat at his desk.

Ahmed tapped on the open door and followed him in. 'Sir.'

'What is it, lad?' the inspector said testily as he riffled through the papers on his desktop.

Tentatively Ahmed said. 'Sir, please tell me, did Hull spit?'

'Spit?' Angel queried.

Ahmed looked abashed. 'Er I mean, er — "come clean"?'

Angel smiled. 'You mean, did he "cough"?' He smiled broadly. 'Yes, Ahmed. He coughed.'

Ahmed beamed. 'Very good, sir. I'm glad for you, sir.'

The policeman stopped smiling. 'I thought I asked you to find DS Gawber for me.'

'Yes, sir.'

'Well, chop-chop! And get out of those clothes!'

Ahmed still beaming closed the inspector's office door.

Angel smiled briefly as he started shuffling through the papers on his desk looking for something. At the bottom of the pile was the postcard size photograph of Lady Yvette Millhouse. That was what he had been looking for. He stared at it closely. It reminded him of the sort of photograph a society beauty of the thirties would have posed for in a professional photographer's studio. And she was wearing the flamboyant jewellery of that period. He remembered that a foreign name was stamped on the back of the photograph. He turned it over. In the form of a sort of a 'logo,' in a circle was the name, 'Marcus La Touche.'

There was a knock on the door.

'Come in.'

It was DS Gawber. 'You wanted me, sir?'

'Yes. Sit down.' Angel said abruptly. 'You're harder to find than Lord Lucan.' He rubbed his chin. 'I want you to crack on with Hull while he's on the boil. I think it'll be a mere formality, now. But it's best to get on with it quickly. I don't want him going cold. He's twitching more than lace curtains in a cul-de-sac. He'll cough his heart up. He'd rather do three years inside than get the wrong side of the Scudamores. And his wife, Ingrid, is a close friend of Edie Scudamore,' he chuckled.

Gawber grinned. 'Yes, Ahmed told me.'

'But you've got to sew it up, Ron. And quick. I want a case as strong as nun's elastic. No loose ends. No surprises in court. You understand?'

DS Gawber nodded and then said, 'Did you find out Hull's accomplice?'

'Yes. It *was* Scott. I should have known it was *one* of the Scudamores.' Angel went straight on quickly. 'Get Hull's solicitor in now. Who is it? Blomfield?'

Ron Gawber nodded. 'And he's smart.'

Then Angel pointed his finger at him. 'Don't worry. Hull's as scared as a long-tailed cat in a roomful of rocking-chairs. He'll not renege. But get him while he's hot. And get it signed, sealed and delivered before you fetch Scott in. Do it now. I want it in the bag before Harry Hull knows what's hit him. And I don't want Scott Scudamore to get wind of what's afoot.'

'Right, sir.' He smiled and turned to the door. Then looked back. 'Someone should take Ahmed home and let him get out of those clothes.'

'I'll see to it.' He sniffed, looked at his hands and turned up his nose. And I need a shower and a clean shirt myself. I feel as mucky as a dog-walker's boot.'

Ron Gawber closed the door.

Angel picked up the phone and tapped out a number. A young voice said, 'Yes? Pathology.'

'Dr Mac, please. It's Michael Angel. He's expecting me.'

'Hold on.'

Angel heard the pathologist clear his throat as he picked up the phone. 'I thought it would be you, Mick. Tell you what I've got so far.'

'Thanks, Mac.'

'Aye, well she has been murdered and it could well be the woman you are looking for,' he sniffed. 'Slim. Soft hands. Well-manicured. No pressure on her feet. Very little muscle tone. No sportswoman. Never done a day's physical work in her life.'

Angel started scribbling in his notebook as the doctor's Glaswegian twang rang in his ear. 'Yes, Mac.'

'Contusions on the throat consistent with her being choked by a person with large hands, almost certainly a man, causing asphyxiation and inhibiting the supply of blood to the brain, resulting in death. Discoloration and bruises to the throat and neck also indicate that she had been wearing jewellery, or some sort of heavily patterned clothing, that would make regular indentations on the neck under pressure, that is, while the assailant was choking her. Her fingernails were freshly damaged so she put up some resistance. She had been dead six to twelve hours and had been left in a horizontal position on her back, probably where she was murdered, before being dumped in Western Beck. Her lungs were bone dry.'

Angel pursed his lips. 'Hmmm. Anything under the fingernails?'

'No.'

'Would her assailant be marked by her?'

'You mean scratched and so on? I shouldn't think so. There was no blood on her nails or her teeth. I suspect the assailant would have hardly noticed her relatively feeble efforts to defend herself.'

Angel grunted. 'Not much to go on, Mac.'

'No. There might be more.'

'Any DNA?'

'No chance.'

'Is she fit to be seen? For ID?'

'Give me an hour. I'll have her made to look presentable.'

'I'll be in with someone from her family, shortly or in the morning. Thanks Mac. I'll buy you a pint.'

He put down the phone and gazed down at the notes he had made.

The sad time had now arrived when it had become necessary to tell Sir Charles Millhouse that there was a strong possibility that his wife had been found dead in Western Beck and to ask him to attend the mortuary to identify the body. This was one of the jobs that Angel would have liked to have avoided.

An hour later, the policeman silently led Sir Charles Millhouse, his son, Duncan, and daughter-in-law, Susan, through a side entrance to Bromersley Hospital, along a short corridor to the door bearing the one stark word 'Mortuary' in black on the glass pane. Angel knocked on the door and walked in. The Millhouse family followed.

The high, long room was white tiled and had an expanse of frosted glass through which the low winter sun shone, casting shadows of the window frames on the opposite tiled wall. The floor was tiled with a network of channels covered by perforated iron grills to allow fluids to drain away. The place reeked of ammonia and antiseptics. A constant throbbing hum could be heard from refrigeration machinery.

At the far end of the room there were two brown painted doors: on one, in black, was the word, 'Private,' and on the other, 'Laboratory.'

A young man in a blue shirt, blue trousers, blue apron, blue hat and white rubber boots was hosing down a stainless-steel trolley at the far end of the room. He recognized Angel, and without a word or change of expression, he turned off the hose and approached the bank of twenty-four large steel drawers, some with paper documents stuck with pink sticking plaster on the front. He waited by one of the drawers.

Inspector Angel glanced back at Sir Charles and his family. With a gesture, he invited them to pass in front of him and go towards the young man. He then followed close behind. Nobody spoke. When they were all gathered by the technician, Angel gave the man a discreet nod. The technician gently pulled out a drawer about three feet only and then withdrew to a discreet distance. The refrigeration machinery droned louder.

A swirl of odourless cold vapour drifted from out of the drawer, across a white linen sheet covering the head and shoulders of a corpse and then trickled in wisps downwards to the sides of the drawer and the floor. Everyone gazed down at the cover.

Angel, his face set like stone, looked up at Sir Charles and raised his eyebrows. The man gave an almost imperceptible nod and Angel slowly peeled back the white sheet. The group of four looked down intently at the head and shoulders of the dead woman. Her face was a pale blue colour, except for the eyelids and one corner of her mouth which were red. Apart from several protruding dark blue veins down the neck, her skin was tight and without any wrinkle, blemish or sign of age. Her eyes were closed. Her hair was ordered but uncombed and had been arranged evenly at the sides of the face. Her neck was covered with a white bandage.

Susan Millhouse involuntarily breathed in sharply and reached out to find her husband Duncan's arm. Sir Charles put a hand up to his mouth and fingered his lower lip.

* * *

Ahaz knocked on Angel's office door.

'Come in.'

'Mrs Moore, Sir,' Ahmed said and showed a lady of about sixty years of age into the inspector's office.

Angel immediately put down his pen, stood up and extended his hand to the lady.

'Ah. Come in, Mrs Moore.'

He shook her hand. It was like shaking a piece of wet fish.

'Pleased to meet you, sir,' she said mechanically.

'Thank you for coming to the station.'

'It's nothing. As I said on the phone, I was coming into town anyway.'

'Please sit down,' he indicated the chair nearest his desk. 'I am Detective Inspector Angel. This is Cadet Ahaz.'

Ahmed smiled at the lady and then raised his eyebrows in an inquiring way across at the policeman. 'Close the door and sit over there, Ahmed.'

58

Angel forced a smile at the plumpish but attractive lady in a grey raincoat who leaned down from the chair to put her large handbag on the floor.

'This is purely informal, Mrs Moore.'

The lady shuffled uncomfortably into the chair and looked intently at him.

'Firstly, I'd like to say how sorry I am that Lady Millhouse has died, and that it is necessary for me to have to ask you these questions,' he said, as he opened his leather-backed notebook.

'I perfectly well understand, Inspector,' she sniffed, producing a handkerchief from her pocket. 'It is a great tragedy for Sir Charles and the family and indeed for the town — after all he is their MP. Her ladyship was becoming well known too, you know. She was liked and respected by everyone she met.'

'I'm sure. Perhaps we can start by asking you how long you worked for her ladyship?'

'I worked at the Hall all my life, on and off. I started there straight from school, as housemaid to Sir Charles's father. I was there when young Sir Charles was born, when he went away to school; when he went to university and then when he went into the army. Then, when I was twenty, I got married and I left to have a baby. I had a little girl. Anyway, when she was five, the first Sir Charles's mother, Lady Amanda, asked me to come back. Which I did. I was very glad to. We needed the money. My husband wasn't really very well paid.'

'What did your husband do?'

'He worked at the Hall. He's always worked at the Hall. Went there as an apprentice, then he worked his way up. He was an undergardener to Old Bloombury. A real tyrant he was!'

'Old Bloombury is the head gardener?'

59

'Not now, sir. Passed away about ten years ago. My husband is head gardener now. Actually, he's the *only* gardener now. He does the work that four men did. I don't know why he stays. Mind you, they do have contractors in to cut all the grass. And a specialist firm to look after the lake and the fish. But he can't keep it to the standard it was in Sir Charles's father's day. He's told young Sir Charles that to his face. His reply was, "Well, do the best you can." And he does. Those gardens and grounds was a picture. Like a picture postcard.' She sniffed and applied a handkerchief.

'I'll need to speak to your husband very soon. Would you ask him to get in touch with me?'

'Of course, I will, Inspector. He'll help all he can, I know that.'

'Please carry on.'

She continued. 'It's not that they are generous with the pay at the Hall. They never were. But it was nice work. And people used to visit and stay overnight many a time. And some of them used to tip most handsomely. Some were very nice, but not all. Of course, I'm talking about the days when there were up to four regular kitchen staff and downstairs maids and an upstairs maid and everything. I mean it'll never be the same again.' She shook her head. 'They don't entertain hardly at all now. That sort of petered out when old Sir Charles and Lady Amanda died. Although young Sir Charles and his first wife did have a regular visitor — a friend — who would stay overnight or for a few days. Perhaps a weekend or so. He was a very nice gentleman, very wealthy, a banker I think he was. Came up from London. Stayed a lot, on and off, for a year or more. Very respectable. Always on his own. Finished up in some sort of trouble though. It was in all the papers. I forget what it was all about. You wouldn't think such a nice man could find himself in trouble. Nothing dirty. I mean nothing scandalous. It was to do with drinking, I think. He was supposed to have had too much to drink and finished up in some sort of car accident. I never properly understood it. Anyway, Sir Charles and his wife stopped inviting him, I think, or he stopped coming. It all seemed to happen at once. He was always the perfect gentleman to me, and I never heard a bad word said about him by any of the staff. But I suppose that's life. But speak as you find, I say. He was ever so nice. And everybody got at least a pound note from him every time he stayed. And that was in the days when you could buy something worthwhile with a pound. I could get a nice pair of stockings with it and have some change. *That* was before decimalisation. I always said—'

'I'm sorry to interrupt, Mrs Moore—'

'Oh,' she replied with a start. 'I'm talking too much. I'm sorry, Inspector. My husband is always saying—'

'Not at all. It's all very interesting,' he said smiling. 'Just for my notes . . . What was the name of the gentleman?' Angel asked gently.

Mrs Moore paused for a second and looked upwards. 'A sort of foreign name. La Touche. Yes that's right. Mr La Touche.'

Angel's eyebrows raised and his eyes opened wide. 'Mr La Touche, did you say?'

Mrs Moore noticed his interest. 'You know him, Inspector?'

Angel shook his head, and truthfully said, 'No.' But his memory had immediately flown to the imprint on the back of that photograph of Lady Yvette Millhouse.

Mrs Moore continued, unperturbed by the inspector's obvious interest in the name. 'And do you know, that Mr La Touche used to arrive in a yellow Rolls Royce and dressed in a black coat and pin-striped trousers. Very smart he looked too. And he always wore a hat. A black Homburg, I think it was.'

She noticed the policeman writing prolifically and at speed. She stopped, looked down at the notepad and said, 'Shall I go on?'

'Please do,' Angel replied without looking up. 'What can you tell me about the young Sir Charles's first wife?'

Mrs Moore took a deep breath. 'Well, she was very nice. Very beautiful. She and Sir Charles were very happy . . . as far as you could see.'

She paused.

'You were living in at the Hall at this time, weren't you?'

'Yes.'

'You would see a lot of the young couple then? Tell me what you know of their relationship. Was it a happy marriage?'

'Oh yes. It seemed to be, Inspector. It was her early death that was so awful.' She shuddered.

Angel looked up at her. 'Death is always awful. What was so different about her death?'

'So young!'

'Yes, of course. How old was she?'

'Forty, I believe.'

'And what did she die of?'

'Well, there were various reasons given at the time. The newspapers were full of all sorts of wild ideas. At the coroners' court, the verdict given was that she died of natural causes. Well, that was good enough for me. You can't get more reliable information than that, can you? The papers seemed to think that young Sir Charles had a reason to want her ladyship's death. Outrageous, I call it! There was talk, and I believe it was only talk, that he was having an affair with a young lady in London. And then there was all that to do with Mr La

Touche. And then there was Mr La Touche's death shortly after that.'

Angel scribbled away. 'And was anybody's name connected with Sir Charles?'

Mrs Moore sneered. 'Only models. Glamour pusses. People we'd never heard of up here.'

'Any particular name?' He persisted gently.

'I think it was all talk, Inspector. I really do.'

Angel smiled at her.

'You don't remember any particular person, by name, I mean?'

'As I said, Inspector, it was all talk. I never knew no names.'

He would have to be content with that for now, he thought. He continued.

'And when did Mr La Touche die?'

'Oh, we seemed to be doing nothing but run to the Church and the crematorium about that time. Everything seemed to be happening at once! First young Charles married. Shortly after that Baby Duncan was born. He was baptized. The following year, old Sir Charles and Lady Amanda died within a few months of each other. There was a gap of about ten years or more and then Mr La Touche died, and young Charles's first wife shortly after that.'

'What can you tell me about life at the Hall immediately prior to Lady Yvette's disappearance?'

'Well, they didn't entertain much, and staff that either left or retired weren't replaced. That coincided with when my mother was ill. My husband and me went to live with her to keep an eye on her and that. And we stopped living in at the Hall. There's only me to cook and clean for them there now. Young Sir Charles was in London a lot, and her ladyship used to tidy round and keep things shipshape. They would dine out a lot at weekends unless they had visitors. I don't know what'll happen now. But, if you ask me, everything wants a good bottoming.'

Angel pursed his lips.

'Was everything harmonious? Did Sir Charles and Lady Yvette get on well together?'

'Oh, yes. Like two lovebirds, they was. And she hardly ever left him when he was ill.'

Angel looked up. 'Was he ill often?'

'Hardly ever. He went through his measles and his mumps and that when he was young. But no. He was never ill really. He'd the constitution of a horse. Not until about a month ago. He had a bout of something. He kept vomiting. And sometimes it showed blood. Well, her ladyship nearly went mad with worry. He went into that posh hospital near Leeds to have tests. They shove a camera down your throat and have a good look round. She stuck to him like glue throughout all this. Anyway, he came home and seemed all right for a few days. But then it started all over again. He went back into hospital, and that's how it was for a bit. Her ladyship was that worried. I caught her in tears more than once. She never said what it was . . . and he didn't.'

'Does he seem to be all right now, Mrs Moore?'

'Oh yes. Eats and drinks what he likes. I think he drinks too much. It's the whisky. He doesn't know when to stop. His father used to tell him he drank too much. But these young ones takes no notice. Her ladyship was a good influence on him. But he knew how to get round her. He was always bringing her flowers and presents and that. But he was away a lot, mind. He sits in Parliament, you know. He'd leave late on Sunday or early on Monday morning, depending. But he'd be back late on Friday or earlier if he could get away. He began to be very nervous at leaving her. He was very worried I remember, after the burglary.'

Angel looked up. His eyes opened wide. 'Burglary?'

'Oh yes. I thought you'd know all about that. Your chaps was all over the place. They asked me a lot of questions. Anyone would have thought I'd something to do with it.'

'I'm sure they didn't.' He smiled reassuringly. 'When was this, Mrs Moore?'

'About two months ago.'

Angel resumed his writing. 'Do you remember who dealt with it?'

She shook her head. 'No. But they would be from here, I suppose.'

'I'll look into it. Thank you, Mrs Moore.'

'They took a lot of the old silver from off the sideboard, and some jewellery from her ladyship's bedroom.'

'Was she in the house at the time?'

'Yes. But she never heard a thing. It made her very nervous, though. It was shortly after that, Sir Charles had that expensive burglar alarm system and the extra outside lights put in. They come on when you pass them.'

'Yes. Yes.'

'And those bells used to drive me batty!'

Angel raised his eyebrows quizzically.

Mrs Moore put her hands to her ears to demonstrate. 'When they were installing them. Them men used to ring them on and off, on and off, all day. Testing they said it was. They drove me mad! Then there is the buzzers. They buzz when anybody walks on the portico. At night the lights go on. It's like the Edingborough Tattoo when them lights go on.'

'Oh, I see. And did anything unusual happen the Friday her ladyship went missing?'

Mrs Moore paused a second, and then said, firmly, 'No. Nothing. Same as usual, I'm sure.'

'You came in — at what time?'

'Nine o'clock as usual. Friday's is normally a tidying round day for me. See that everything was shipshape for when Sir Charles arrived back. Her ladyship used to go down the shops. She was back, loaded up with groceries and whatever. Everything as usual. She paid me and my husband at four o'clock and we left.'

'And everything was as usual.'

'Yes.'

Angel looked her straight in the eye. 'You realize that you may very well have been the last person to see her ladyship alive.'

Mrs Moore dabbed her nose with the handkerchief, then nodded.

'Tell me, what was she wearing. Can you recall?'

She nodded again. 'She was wearing a thick woollen red jumper and blue jeans, and brown leather shoes.'

'A wristwatch? Any jewellery?'

Mrs Moore nodded enthusiastically. 'Yes. Yes. A small very neat square-faced watch — she always wore that. And her pearls. She wouldn't be without her pearls.'

'Pearls?' Angel queried.

'A choker of small creamy coloured pearls. They were graduated and made into a beautiful fancy pattern. They were antique of course. She did love them. Sir Charles bought them for her, of course. She nearly always wore them.'

'Were they valuable, Mrs Moore?'

'I really don't know. Being her ladyship, I 'spect they were. I know she liked wearing them. Maybe she treasured them because they were one of the few items not taken by the burglars, when they had that break in.'

Angel nodded as he stroked his chin. He wrote something in big letters in his notebook. Then he looked into her moist eyes and said, 'Tell me, Mrs Moore. This could be very important. There was absolutely nothing different or unusual in what you did, how her ladyship was, her attitude to you, what she may have said to you, her attitude to her husband coming home, absolutely nothing different from the way she usually was on a Friday afternoon? . . . Absolutely nothing?'

She looked him straight back, wiped her nose and said, 'Absolutely nothing, Inspector.'

Angel waited a second. Then he smiled at her, put down his pen and stood up.

'Well thank you very much, Mrs Moore.'

She didn't stir, but her mouth opened and then closed again, and then she said, 'There was *one* thing, Inspector.'

'Oh yes,' Angel said, his eyes brightening. 'And what was that?'

'Well, it was not really anything directly to do with Sir Charles and her ladyship.'

'No?'

'No. It's just that the hearthrug out of the drawing room has gone missing. I noticed it on Monday morning. I mentioned it to Sir Charles. He didn't seem very interested. He said that he'd told you about it, and that it didn't matter. Well I think it matters. If someone upped and took *my* hearthrug, I'd be wanting to know about it. Now who would want to steal a rug, I ask you? They must be very poor. I just thought I would mention it.'

FIVE

Later that afternoon, Detective Inspector Angel was at his desk trying to reduce the pile of paperwork that was swamping him. He was shuffling letters and reports around when the phone rang. He grunted and picked up the receiver.

'Angel.'

It was the WPC on the station exchange. 'Inspector, there's a call for you from a DI Smith in Galashiels CID. I think that's in Scotland, sir.'

Angel smiled. 'Yes, lass. Galashiels is in Scotland. Put him through.'

A broad Scottish voice said, 'Is that the Angel of the North?'

He grinned. 'Now Smithy, don't cheek your elders. How did you get on with that little job I asked you to do for me?'

The loud, cheerful voice said, 'It wasn't easy.'

'I didn't think it would be. Nothing I ever asked you to do for me was easy. If it was easy, I'd do it myself.'

'But we've managed to find out all you wanted, I think.'

'Good. I appreciate it. It would have brightened your day and been a change from apple scrumping, dog's barking and dangerous sheep roaming cases you have to deal with every day.'

DI Smith chuckled. 'At least we don't have to work in that mucky Yorkshire air.'

'It must be very nice up there in Galashiels, I'll give you that. Now tell me, what did you find out?'

The badinage over, DI Smith delivered the information Angel had asked for, and, after promising to visit him when next he was in Scotland, he thanked him profusely.

He replaced the phone, just as the wet, noisy boots of Detective Sergeant Ron Gawber, Scott Scudamore and his solicitor, Mr Blomfield, clattered noisily down the green corridor past his office door.

Angel rose from his desk, quietly opened his office door and peered down the corridor after them. He smiled and nodded. The entry of Scott Scudamore and Blomfield into the interview room established that Ron Gawber had secured the confession to the robbery of Patel's off-licence from Harry Hull and that the policeman was now about to attempt to extract a similar statement from Scott Scudamore. That wasn't going to be easy with Blomfield present. Angel considered a confession a highly unlikely outcome. Nevertheless, he continued to smile. He considered that there was a certain pleasurable satisfaction in the way that case was heading and he had not yet played all the cards in his hand.

He closed the office door, returned to his desk, picked up the phone and pressed a button.

DS Gawber answered. 'Interview room.'

'I know how it is. I've just heard you arrive. You've got Scott Scudamore and Blomfield in there, haven't you? Just answer yes or no.'

'Yes.'

'You couldn't have started yet?'

'No.'

'Good. I just want clarification on a couple of points. Am I right in assuming that Scott Scudamore is still insisting that he wasn't with Harry Hull in the Patel robbery?'

'Yes.'

'And is he still saying he was with Annabell what's her name, that married woman he's living with, all that evening and night?'

'Yes.'

'So if we can break that alibi, have we got him?'

'Yes.'

'Definitely?'

'Definitely!'

'Right, Ron. Well, you see what *you* can do. I want you to keep Scott Scudamore there as long as possible. Spin it out. Go over it again. You know what I mean. I know Blomfield will object, but give me as much time as possible, will you?'

'Right.'

'I'm going out. I'll let you know when I'm back. Good luck, lad. Bye.'

'Goodbye, sir.'

Angel returned the phone to its cradle and reached for his coat and hat.

Ten minutes later, he was driving his car through a very large estate of red brick, blue slate roof, semi-detached houses in a suburb of Bromersley. Some of the house windows were boarded up. He drove slowly along a street looking out for a particular house. He passed two young girls hopping across squares marked out in chalk on the pavement. A little boy was struggling to ride a small, brightly coloured tricycle in the gutter. Three dogs of assorted sizes and colours bounced playfully together from the pavement to the road and back again. Empty crisp and pizza boxes decorated the street. A tin can flew up from under the car wheel, rattled on the prop shaft and ended in the gutter.

Angel found the house he wanted and pulled up. He locked the car door and walked down the concrete path. The small area in the front of the house was a mass of tall grass. It was fenced all round but the front gate was missing. There was no number to be seen on the door or on the wall. He knocked on the flaking green painted door. It was opened promptly by a very slim young woman with long hair. Most of her hair was white but it had a wide, jet-black parting down the middle. She moved one side of her body around the edge of the door. Her skinny, nicotine stained, long fingers grabbed hold of the outside doorknob.

'Yes?' she said in a voice like bagpipes with tonsillitis. If she had been on the Clyde, she would have stopped all the shipping.

Angel removed his hat and forced a smile. 'Mrs Scudamore? Mrs Annabell Scudamore?'

Her jaw dropped. She hung on to the doorknob. And drew her body close to the door edge so that her denim clad knee was slightly bent and wrapped around it.

'Here. I know you. You're a copper.' She spoke as if there was something wrong with the drains.

'Detective Inspector Angel,' he announced, replacing his hat. 'I wonder if I could have a word with Mr Scudamore, Mr Scott Scudamore?'

'Well *he's* not in. Some other copper came up and carted him off to your place to give 'im a statement,' she said with a sniff. She began to slide her body up and down the edge of the door like a fidgety child.

'That's a coincidence,' Angel lied. 'Never mind. 'Perhaps you'll be able to help me.'

'Oh yes?' she drawled, eyeing him uncertainly. 'I'm not answering any more questions. I've already given your lot a statement. And it was in front of our solicitor, Mr Blomfield, so I know it's all right.'

'Oh, is it?'

'Yes it is,' she replied firmly.

Angel stroked his chin. 'You originally came down from Scotland, didn't you?'

She looked at him intently. 'Scotland, Wales, London, Yorkshire. I've been all over.'

'You were a dancer at the Can Can Club, weren't you? Is that what brought you to Bromersley? Is that where you met Scott Scudamore?'

She looked surprised and then pleased. 'I was an exotic dancer then,' she giggled. 'I 'ad my own act, you know. I 'ad my own snake. Travelled around.' She slid up and down the edge of the door again.

'What do you do now, Bella?'

'Nothing.'

'You clear glasses at The Feathers six nights a week, don't you?'

She shrugged. 'What's it to you?'

'But you have family in Scotland somewhere though, don't you? Whereabouts in Scotland, Bella?'

'Mind your own business, copper.'

Angel smiled. 'It's Galashiels.'

She wasn't surprised. 'So what? Yes, it's Galashiels. What's it to you?'

'Married a Scotsman. Had a baby. A little girl, wasn't it?'

Her jaw dropped and she stared at him for a second. That surprised her. 'What's it to you?' she repeated. The thin blue lips of her mouth tightened.

'Nothing at all, Bella.' He paused.

He wasn't sure if his timing was right. He needed to charm her into a pleasant frame of mind. He had to judge the right moment before he could advance.

'Let's see, how old is your little girl now? Five, is it, or six?'

She pursed her lips. 'She's six, and what's it got to do with you?' she replied with a glare.

Angel wished he was inside the house. There was the possibility she could slam the door on him. He wanted to close in. She wasn't warming to him. It wasn't going quite according to plan.

'How do you know about her, anyway?' She asked.

'Why, is it a secret?'

'No. Why? Should it be?'

'No reason. Do you see much of her, Bella?'

Her face changed. The ends of her mouth turned downwards. She said nothing.

Angel persisted. He pursed his lips. 'Do you see much of her?'

She looked down. 'Now and then.'

'She lives with her father in Galashiels, doesn't she? I hear he's a nice respectable fella. He isn't married either. He adores your little girl, doesn't he? His Mum looks after your little girl in the daytime while he's at work. He picks her up in the evenings. And he has her at weekends. Every weekend.'

She shook her head and tightened her jaw. Her long hair rippled over her shoulders. 'I know! I know!'

'Good, steady job, I hear. No chance of being laid off. Job for life. Brings in a good screw as a farm manager,' Angel said quietly.

'So what?' she snarled.

Angel stroked his chin. 'He might have you back,' he added ruefully.

She stopped the gymnastics and stared at him intently.

He decided to take the bull by the horns. He put his hand on the door. 'Perhaps we should go inside.'

She tightened her bony hand around the doorknob. 'It's all right. We can talk out here. It isn't going to take long. Mr . . . er . . . ?'

'Angel,' he prompted.

Her mood changed again. 'Oh yes, Angel,' she said knowingly. She moved her head up and then down very slowly and smirked at him. 'My husband said you were a smarmy so and so.'

Angel looked across at the slim figure.

He smiled. 'I'll take that as a compliment.'

She moved closer to him and smirked. 'You're cheeky. What are you after? You're a cheeky monkey!'

His jaw dropped. He looked her straight in the face. She forced a laugh, throwing back her head and opening wide her small mouth.

Angel blinked at her proximity. She'd more fillings than Heinz had varieties. But she was laughing. Perhaps this was the right moment. He took a chance. He whisked a sheet of paper out from his inside pocket and unfolded it.

'It's about this statement, Bella.'

'What about it?'

He forced a smile. 'Can I ask you a straight question?'

She giggled. 'I don't promise to give you a straight answer.' She started slithering up and down the edge of the open door again.

'That's all right,' he replied lightly. 'This is what you said.' He began to read from the statement. 'Scott was at home all that evening and night. He did not go out at all. He stayed in with me and we watched television and had a cup of tea.'

He lowered the paper, then smiled and shook his head. 'Had a cup of tea?'

Bella grinned. 'Yes. That's right. That's exactly what happened. Exactly.'

He decided it was now or never.

He looked down into her watery, pale, brown eyes, shook his head again and said, 'Why do you lie for him, Bella? You don't have to lie for him. He's not your husband. He doesn't keep you. He doesn't work. He never has done. He's bone idle. He lives off you. He steals and robs. He's no conscience. And what's worse, he terrorises little people.'

Angel waved the statement at her and continued without a pause.

'In this case, an old Pakistani shopkeeper and his wife.'

She stared at him with a face of stone. He could see a vein down her neck throbbing. He spoke stronger and faster.

'Scott Scudamore isn't worth a paper frying pan. Why don't you dump him while you've still got your looks? You've got a man in Galashiels. A hardworking, reliable, dependable fella. And you've a beautiful, adorable little girl. And yet you hang around with this drip Scott, a certain candidate for a long stretch in Maidstone — take my word for it. Yet you know damned well that every Saturday night, he goes to the Can Can Club with his brothers Scrap and Barry, when they're not locked up, and afterwards, while you're sweating, collecting glasses at The Feathers, he's with a tart in Scrap's flat and—'

Suddenly, without warning, Bella let go of the doorknob, slipped inside the house and slammed the door shut with a mighty bang. He heard the key turn in the lock.

'Damn!' He had been afraid of that happening all along.

He stood a few seconds looking at the locked door and gave a heavy sigh. He turned around, folded Bella's statement and put it back into his inside pocket, and licking his lips, walked up the path to his car.

He didn't even glance at the house as he started the engine. He slammed it in gear, let in the clutch and it stalled. He bared his teeth and turned the ignition key again. The engine roared into life. He put the car into gear, let in the clutch again and glided quickly through the sprawling estate.

When he was back on the main road driving back to the station, he opened the glove compartment and started fumbling around inside it. There was a duster, an old AA book, a tyre tread gauge, a pair of handcuffs, a sign with the word 'POLICE' printed on it for use in certain on duty situations, but no cigarettes. The search was in vain. He closed the compartment door with a bang and began fumbling in the pocket in the car door. There were none there either.

Fifteen minutes later, he was back at his desk in the police station. He lifted the phone. 'Is it a bad moment, Ron?'

'No, sir,' DS Gawber said. Angel thought he sounded tired. 'In fact, Mr Blomfield and Mr Scudamore are both ready to leave.'

'I bet they are. Is there anything you can hold Scott on?'

'No.'

Angel's voice dropped. 'Oh. Right. See them off, then come into my office.'

He replaced the phone. He leaned back in his chair, stretched his arms above his head and grunted. He arched his back and sighed. Then suddenly he reached forward, picked up the phone again and pressed a button.

The familiar voice of Ahmed said, 'CID office. Cadet Ahaz speaking.'

'What are you doing, lad?' Angel growled.

'Nothing, sir.'

'Nothing! Well, you should be. Where do you think you are? On your holidays!' And before the cadet had time to reply, he added, 'Bring three teas and yourself in here pronto.'

He slammed the phone down.

There was a knock on the door.

'Come in.'

It was Ron Gawber.

Angel looked up at him.

The sergeant didn't speak and didn't smile. Angel pointed to the chair. 'No luck?'

Ron Gawber pulled a face, shook his head and sat down. He pushed a statement form in front of the inspector. 'He's sly.'

Angel lifted up the paper and without looking at it said, 'Is it the same as before?'

'Yes sir. I couldn't move him an inch.'

'Didn't think you would,' he replied bluntly, dropping the paper on his desk. 'While you were having another go at Scott, I've been to see Bella!' he announced proudly.

Gawber looked up brightly. 'Aaah!'

Angel sighed. 'She wouldn't let me in. If she had let me into the house, who knows? I should have taken it more slowly. And, just, maybe . . .' He floundered.

'Perhaps give it another go? Tomorrow? Or in a day or two?'

Angel shook his head. 'No. I should have insisted on going in the house or threatened to leave. If I had handled it like that, her curiosity would have got the better of her and she would have let me in. Then I would have stalled and dithered. She would have offered me a cup of tea. You know, to keep me there. I should have played it out.'

Gawber watched him closely.

He went on. 'Instead, I rushed it. I wanted to get back. Agreed to talk to her on the doorstep. So when I reached the bit she didn't like, she slammed the door on me. Women don't tick like men. She got angry with herself — well that's all right. It's all right to let *them* feel guilty. They sometimes like it. It can be a release. But it doesn't do for them to dislike the one that's *telling* them.'

He had almost forgotten he was with Ron Gawber. It was as if he was talking to himself. Then he looked up. 'I should have sent you.' He grinned. 'You're prettier. But she is hard, Ron. Harder than Herod on heroin!'

Gawber shook his head. 'I didn't do any good with Scudamore. I didn't get him to change *one* word! With Blomfield there, it was almost predictable. They sat in silence most of the time. They let me go rambling on.'

'Of course it was predictable,' Angel said. 'But sometimes, you've got to go through the motions.'

There was a slight pause.

'You let him and Blomfield understand that we didn't believe him, didn't you?'

Gawber smiled. 'You bet.'

Angel nodded approvingly. 'There'll be a bit of a stir going on between Scott and Bella now then! And Scott'll be getting the rough end of it. You never know. I just might have unsettled their cosy relationship. I might have stirred her conscience. And you might have pressured Scott enough to make him nervous. All this stress might be working on them as we speak. You never know.'

'I hope it happens sooner rather than later, sir.'

'It might, Ron, it might.'

There was a knock on the door.

'Come in.'

It was Ahmed with the tea.

Angel licked his lips. 'I'm drier than Chief Constable's annual review.'

Ahmed passed the tray round.

Angel helped himself and then looking at Ahmed said, 'Sit down over there.'

Ahmed took the chair by the wall.

There was a short pause as the three of them sipped the tea.

Ron Gawber said, 'Where are we now then, sir?'

Not seeming to hear him, with a twinkle in his eye, Angel said, 'Do you know, Sergeant. This cadet has nothing to do.'

Gawber smiled.

'I am *not* on my holidays. I have plenty to do, sir,' he said earnestly.

'You told me you were doing nothing!' the inspector said.

'I meant that what I was doing would not be more important than whatever you would want me to do for you, sir.'

'Well, what *were* you doing?'

'Filing, sir.'

Angel's eyebrows lifted. 'Filing?'

Ahmed nodded.

'Your nails?' Angel growled, hiding a smile.

'No, sir,' Ahmed said quickly. 'Police files. The "wanted," and the daily reports, sir.'

'Oh.'

Angel sipped the tea.

'Well, there's nothing more we can do with the Patel case.' He said rubbing his chin. 'We will have to give the last round to Scott Scudamore. We've got Harry Hull, at least. He'll get at least two years. We'll have to be content with that, for now.'

The inspector riffled through some papers on his desk, as he spoke.

'Tell me, who arrived first at Western Beck, did you?'

'Yes, sir.'

'Any sign of tyre tracks?'

'No, sir.'

'And who found the body?'

'An angler, out for a day's sport. I've got his name. It's in my report.'

'And you had a good look round the area where she was found. In the weeds on the bank?'

The sergeant nodded.

'The divers find anything?'

'No. No weapon. There was nothing only rubbish . . . part of an old pram, half submerged, a rubber tyre, an old carpet. The usual junk.'

Angel's eyes flashed. He turned to face him. 'An old carpet? An old carpet? That might be the one we're looking for.'

Ron Gawber looked surprised. 'An old carpet?'

'Yes. Get it. Get it now. Let Mac have it. I'll tell him to expect it.'

The sergeant's jaw dropped. 'Yes, sir.' He stood up to leave.

'Just a minute.'

Angel quickly looked through the pile of papers on his desk. He pulled out a bundle of pages fastened at the corner with a staple. It was Doctor Mac's report on the body dragged out of Western Beck. He waved it at DS Gawber.

'Have you read this?'

'Yes, sir. My copy is in my office.'

'The body *is* Lady Millhouse.'

Gawber nodded. 'Why naked? Mac says there was no apparent sexual interference.'

The phone rang.

The sergeant stood up. 'I'll get that carpet, sir.'

'Hang on. See what this is.'

The inspector lifted the receiver. 'Angel.'

The girl on switchboard said, 'It's Grey's the Undertaker for you, sir.'

'Aye. Put him through, love.' He looked up at Gawber, nodded and pointed a thumb at the door. 'You get off, Ron.'

Gawber nodded and made for the door closing it quietly behind him.

'Good afternoon, Inspector. It's John Grey,' said the obsequious voice down the phone.

'Yes, John?'

'I was wanting to know if we can go ahead with the interment of the remains of the late Lady Millhouse, Inspector?'

'I don't see why not. You'll need to clear it with the coroner's office, Mr Grey. If he'll release the body, it'll be all right with me.'

'Thank you very much, Inspector. Thank you for your cooperation. I will contact the coroner and inform the bereaved directly.'

'The Police always wish to cooperate. By the way, Mr Grey, when you have the date and time of the funeral, would you be certain to let me know? We are not friends of the family, but we must send some flowers, mustn't we?'

'Most charming, Mr Angel. Most delightful. Of course I will, personally.'

'Thank you. Goodbye.'

He replaced the receiver.

'He's as smarmy as an MP at election time.'

He turned to Ahmed still seated quietly by the wall, and, sticking out his chin said, portentously, 'That's a funeral we won't miss!'

Ahmed's big eyes opened wider. 'Yes, sir. Er, I mean, no, sir.'

SIX

Angel was becoming rapidly aware that he was making slow progress with the Millhouse case. Time was not on his side. Although he was happy that definite advancement with the Pakistani off-licence robbery and assault had been made, he was far behind with the investigation of the murder of Lady Yvette Millhouse. Prompt action was to be taken.

At nine o'clock the following morning, he was seated in the plush drawing room at Millhouse Hall with Sir Charles. The large imitation log gas-fired fire roared in front of them and Mrs Moore had placed a large pot of coffee on the table between them.

'Will there be anything else, sir?' She called to Sir Charles Millhouse from the door.

'No. That's fine,' he replied, forcing a smile.

'Thank you, Mrs Moore,' Angel called with a wave.

She nodded and closed the door.

Sir Charles was fully dressed and had a red, silk dressing-gown over his shirt and slacks. He looked relaxed and more at ease than he had been at the police station the week previously.

'Now then, Inspector, I'm all yours.' He said with a big wave of his arm. 'You know my housekeeper then?'

'I interviewed her at the station on Wednesday.'

'Oh, yes.'

The inspector turned over the pages in his small leather-bound notebook and said dourly, 'I have to tell you, Sir Charles, that, as yet, I have not been able to discover a single motive for the murder of your wife. I can find no reason why she should have been murdered. It is very unusual to find someone as universally well liked as your wife was. Are you able to tell me who would have wanted to do away with her?'

Sir Charles stretched his long legs out in front him. His hands were clasped together. He shook his bowed head. 'I cannot, Inspector. I have racked my brain over and over again, but no explanation comes to mind. Everybody loved her. You can't find anyone who has one word to say against her. It's a tragedy, a great tragedy. It's a great personal loss as well.'

'Of course. Of course.' There was a short pause, then Angel said, 'I suppose your son, Duncan, inherits all of your estate now?'

'Well, yes. As a matter of fact, he does,' Sir Charles said, as if he had only just thought of it. Then his jaw tightened. He shook his head. 'There's no point in looking in that direction for a murderer, Inspector. Duncan hasn't got it in him, and besides that, he and Yvette got on extremely well.'

'We have to consider all possibilities, sir.' Angel spoke gently. 'As a matter of record, where were you a week last Saturday and Sunday?'

Sir Charles looked up with raised eyebrows. 'Here. I had some constituents to see in town on Saturday morning. But,

I was here, in the house all day Sunday until about six o'clock when I left for London. I have a flat there.'

'Can anyone verify that, sir?'

'Look here, Inspector,' Sir Charles began to protest.

'I know it may seem unnecessary, but for the record . . . ?'

Sir Charles ran his hand through his hair. 'I am sure my chauffeur can verify that, Inspector,' he replied with a grunt. Then he added, 'You've already seen her. She was here the night you came for that photograph.'

'I'll need to interview her.'

'Of course. I'll tell her to get in touch.'

'Thank you, sir. It will save time.'

'Have you found out how my wife died yet, Inspector?'

'Yes, sir. She was asphyxiated. Strangled almost certainly by a man,' Angel said quietly.

There was a pause.

'How do you know it was a man?'

'We don't. The bruises on the throat are consistent with the size of a man's hands.'

Sir Charles did not reply. He shook his head slowly. 'She didn't drown then?'

'No, sir. Her lungs had no water in them. In fact, we know that a few hours elapsed between her death and her body being dumped in Western Beck.'

'How do you know that?'

Angel hesitated. 'Are you sure you want to hear this, sir?'

After a second's hesitation, Sir Charles said, 'yes'.

Angel pursed his lips and pressed on. 'At death, the heart stops pumping. Circulation of the blood stops, and the simple laws of gravity take over. Blood falls to the lowest part of the body. If left over a certain time in one position, the blood will begin to coagulate. The postmortem indicates that your wife was on her stomach for some time before she reached the reservoir. When in the water, your wife was found floating on her back. It is usual for women in such circumstances to float on their backs.'

Sir Charles said nothing. He remained seated with his long legs outstretched towards the fire. His hands clasped and his head bowed.

'And we have not found any trace of your wife's clothes,' Angel added after a short pause.

Angel noticed the long-cased clock for the first time, ticking in the far corner of the room.

Sir Charles sighed and anticipating his next question said, 'No, Inspector. I do not know what she was wearing.'

Angel decided not to pursue the question. He would ask Mrs Moore who (except for the murderer) appeared to have been the last person to have seen Yvette Millhouse alive.

'I have a few other questions I would like to ask you,' Angel ventured.

'Very well. Let's get them out of the way.'

'About your first wife, I've had a word with the doctor who was looking after her, and he confirms that she died from natural causes. I understand that she was not ill for long?'

Sir Charles sighed and replaced his coffee cup on the table. 'She had not complained of any illness. She died in the garden. It was very sudden. I'm assured that she didn't suffer in the slightest, which was a comfort.'

'And I wondered what effect it had had on your son, Duncan?'

He put his hand to his forehead. 'Of course, Duncan and I were very badly hit. The boy was twenty and away at university. It could have been worse. He could have *found* her. His mother and he were close. Indeed the three of us were very close. We were a very happy family.'

Sir Charles poured the coffee into the two cups. 'But that was five years ago, Inspector. What relevance has that to the death of Yvette?'

Angel gave the slightest shrug, pursed his lips and then said, 'Sometimes one death relates to another. I just want to get the overall picture.'

Sir Charles eased himself forward in his chintz covered armchair and said, 'I don't see any comparison between the two deaths. Surely, one was natural and one was murder?'

'Yes, sir.' Angel was satisfied to let the observation go as evident, at least, for the time being.

Sir Charles shook his head.

The inspector went on. 'And did you know your late wife long before you married her?'

Sir Charles's jaw dropped. 'Not long. No.' He leaned forward and looked the policeman square in the eye. 'Look here, Inspector, are you wanting a complete run down of my private life?'

Angel returned the stare. 'I'm investigating a very serious and unpleasant murder. I'm not at all interested in your private life, sir; only inasmuch as it concerns your wife's death.'

Sir Charles eased back in his chair. He ran his hand across his mouth as he considered the policeman's attitude and his reaction to it.

Angel eased back a little. 'I need to know something of your wife's background. Where she comes from. Who may have been interested in seeing her murdered. I am sorry if my questions upset you, but the information may be vital. I'm sure you see that.'

'I too would like to know who murdered her, and why,' Sir Charles said grimly. 'It doesn't make sense.' He hesitated and then nodded. 'Well, Inspector, Yvette was from a French family. From her photograph you will have seen how beautiful she was. She had been a model and had worked for a French women's magazine. She spoke perfect English. She came to live in London last year. When I met her she was an interpreter. In my work in the House, from time to time, I needed an interpreter. The agency sent her along. I invited her for a meal. I was very lonely. I'd lived like a monk for five years. After a few weeks, I proposed to her. We were married in August.' He shrugged. 'The rest, as they say, is history.'

'I shall need to speak with her relatives. Where can they be contacted?'

'Both her parents were dead. She had no brothers or sisters. She used to get the occasional letter from Paris . . . a woman friend . . . of long-standing, I think. I can't remember the name.'

'Definitely a woman?'

'Yes.'

'And you have never met her?'

'No. I don't even know who it is.'

Angel scribbled something in his notebook. 'We must find her. Perhaps we could look through her correspondence?'

'Of course.' Sir Charles waved a hand towards a big writing bureau positioned against the wall between two huge windows facing the long drive. 'My wife's correspondence was all in there. Help yourself, Inspector.'

Angel put down his coffee cup and went over to the piece of furniture and pulled down the front. He quickly searched the pigeonholes and drawers. There were no letters and no address book. Sir Charles remained seated by the fire.

'There's nothing useful here, sir. Is there any other place she may have kept her letters or addresses?'

Sir Charles looked mystified. 'No, Inspector. That is strange.'

Angel shook his head. 'Well, if you come across the information, please let me know.'

'Yes, of course.'

The inspector returned to the armchair and picked up his leather-bound notebook.

Sir Charles recrossed his long legs, ran a hand through his hair, looked at his wristwatch and said, 'Is this going to take much longer, Inspector? I *am* a Member of Parliament, you know. I *am* expected in London. I shall have to leave soon.'

Angel sighed. 'Well, sir, I suppose we can leave matters there for the time being.' He closed his notebook and slipped it into his inside pocket.

'Good.'

'I mustn't put any unnecessary strain on you. By the way, how are you? Are you keeping well?'

'Very kind of you to ask, Inspector. I am, naturally enough, missing my wife, but I am coping. I had an ulcer recently but I am glad to say that I do believe it's all cleared up now.'

Angel smiled. 'Good. I'm very glad to hear it,' he said and stood up.

Sir Charles reached behind the settee to the telephone on the sofa table and picked up the handset. 'Will you see yourself out? Do you mind?'

'Not at all, sir.' The policeman nodded, crossed the room and opened the drawing room door.

'Thank you, Inspector. And believe me, I appreciate all you're doing,' he added as he dialled a number.

'Only doing my job, sir,' Angel said as he closed the door quietly.

Then, still holding the doorknob on the outside, he over-heard Sir Charles speak into the phone, 'Melanie, it's me . . . Right. We're leaving for London. Pick me up straight away.'

Angel nodded and turned away from the door.

* * *

The detective inspector drove his car into the only vacant space in the private car park at the side of a block of shops and offices located in a commercial area on the outskirts of Leeds. It was a pseudo-Elizabethan building with black painted wooden beams and whitewashed stucco plasterwork decorating the upper half, with nineteen thirties red brick forming the ground floor.

He parked next to a black Mercedes, the car he had last seen outside Millhouse Hall three nights earlier. Its owner was Duncan Millhouse.

He walked briskly round the front of the building and only then noticed that, sharing the ground floor of the building there were three other antique shops, a cafe, an office supplies retailer and a tobacconist. The smell of tobacco wafted briefly to his nostrils as he passed the open shop door. He glanced to the side and saw the shop hadn't any customers. His instinct was to stop, turn back and call in for some cigarettes, but he swiftly turned to his front, tightened his mouth and accelerated towards the door of 'Northern Antiques'.

The shop only had a small frontage, located at the end corner site furthest from the car park. At the side of the door was the only window. Above it was painted in white on a black background, 'Northern Antiques.' He noticed that metal grilles were fitted and padlocked across all the glass. A few colourful Victorian vases, dishes, a barometer, a shapely three-piece silver tea service and a print of a painting of a man in a boat were displayed on the bare wood window bottom. Grubby cardboard poster cards printed black on white that read, 'We pay cash for all genuine antiques,' 'Best prices paid,' and 'Cash waiting,' were placed conspicuously around the window and the door. Beyond the uncovered back of the window he could see furniture stacked tightly, piece upon piece, some with intricately made curved chair legs sticking up in the air and handsome cabinet door handles showing through bits of carpet and drapes used to protect the furniture surfaces that occupied most of the floor of the shop. A profusion of animals' heads on wooden plinths, pictures, barometers and mirrors were hanging haphazardly almost covering the whitewashed walls. A glass topped illuminated counter, a rolled top desk, a swivel chair and a tall stool almost filled the remaining floor space. There was a doorway partly covered with a tatty bead curtain at the back of the shop. A man reading a newspaper was leaning against the arch. He was wearing a trilby hat and had a dead cigarette end hanging from his lips.

Angel could see the back of the head of Duncan Millhouse seated at the roll-top desk, and Susan Millhouse perched on the tall stool. She was wearing a tight red knitted figure-hugging dress and her long legs were entwined round the cross supports and legs of the stool which was behind the illuminated glass topped counter. She took a long suck at the cigarette she held at the end of her fingers and blew a big cloud of smoke into the air.

Angel put his hand on the door handle and walked in. He heard the delicate eastern sound of chimes tinkle over his head.

The faces of the three occupants looked up. The chimes fell silent as he closed the door.

Duncan Millhouse swivelled round in his chair and looked across at the big policeman. He didn't recognize him. He turned back to the desk and carried on writing.

The man reading the newspaper lifted his eyelids briefly in the direction of the inspector and then returned to reading the paper.

Susan Millhouse was the only one of the three who acknowledged his arrival. She switched on her best smile and said, 'Can I help you?'

'Detective Inspector Angel,' he said quietly.

'Of course it is,' she replied with a glossy, carmine smile and, putting the lipstick marked cigarette she was smoking on the ashtray on top of the showcase, untangled herself from the high stool and turned to her husband.

'Duncan.'

'Oh, yes,' the man said, standing up and turning round to face the policeman as he pulled on his suit coat that had been draped on the back of the chair. 'To what do we owe the pleasure?'

From his expressionless tone, Angel didn't think that Duncan Millhouse really thought his visit was a pleasure at all.

The man, who had been leaning against the arch reading the newspaper, rolled round the archway through the bead curtain and disappeared into the back area of the shop.

Duncan straightened his suit coat and pulled his tie into position.

Angel looked down at him. He was one of those men who would always look unkempt even after climbing out of a bath and into expensive, bespoke clothes.

Angel looked around the little shop. His eyes alighted on the glass topped showcase counter so closely attended by Susan Millhouse. It was sparsely filled with old jewellery in old jewellery boxes. He saw a pair of emerald and diamond earrings and a large emerald and diamond ring similar to those he had seen on the photograph of Lady Yvette Millhouse.

'Mmm. Are those earrings and that ring emeralds and diamonds?'

Susan Millhouse looked at her husband and then at Angel and said, 'Yes, Inspector.'

He looked straight at her. 'They look familiar.'

'Oh?' she replied.

Duncan stepped in quickly. 'They were my stepmother's. Yvette wanted us to sell them for her.'

Angel nodded. 'I see.'

Then he looked down at Duncan. 'Is there anywhere we can talk?'

'Yes. Sure.' Millhouse replied hesitantly. 'We can go in the back, I suppose. It's not very comfortable.'

He pushed through the scruffy curtain and called. 'Tom!'

The man who had been reading the newspaper appeared from behind a high stack of big dark stained and varnished chairs and tables. He nodded and shuffled through the curtain into the shop, carrying the newspaper and still bearing the finished cigarette end between his lips. He coughed a few times, turned away from Angel and put his hand to his mouth as he passed by. He took up a position on the high stool by the glass topped showcase.

Millhouse held the curtain back. 'If you would come on through, Inspector? Tom'll be all right. Susie you'd better come, too.'

Angel led the way. Susan Millhouse followed.

There were no seats. There was more furniture carefully wrapped and stacked high all around them. There was a little table in the corner with a kettle, several beakers, a jar of coffee and a part bottle of milk on a tin tray on top of it. A small fireplace with a small electric fire on the cream and brown tiled hearth was conveniently placed to burn the shins.

'This is as private as it gets, Inspector,' Millhouse said.

Angel pursed his lips. 'It won't take long, sir. I need to know where you were last Friday afternoon and evening — when your stepmother went missing.'

'We were here and then at home.'

'Yes, we were here and then at home, Inspector,' Susan Millhouse echoed.

'All the time?'

'Yes,' Duncan said, and his wife nodded.

'Did anybody see you? Did you have any visitors?'

'No. But Dad phoned.'

Angel smiled.

Millhouse licked his lips. 'I don't suppose that counts.'

Angel took out his notebook and pen. 'What time would that be, sir?'

Duncan looked at his wife and then at the policeman. 'I suppose about six o'clock. He was beginning to get worried about Yvette not being there. He asked me if I had any idea where she might be. Of course, I knew nothing, and told him so.'

'When did you last see your stepmother?'

Millhouse screwed up his eyes.

Susan Millhouse said, 'It must have been the previous Friday evening. We often went up to the Hall to see Pa and Yvette on a Friday evening.'

'And you went up last Friday evening, as usual?'

'Yes.'

'You've no idea, either of you, who disliked, hated even, your stepmother, to have wanted to murder her?'

'No.'

An electric bell high on the wall started ringing piercingly. Angel looked up at it.

'That's Tom. Ringing the security bell. Must have a customer,' Millhouse said.

The bell stopped ringing as Duncan held back the curtain across the doorway and peered into the shop. When he saw who it was, he bustled quickly through the arch up to the big man, who was carrying a plastic supermarket shopping bag. Duncan spoke urgently and softly to the visitor.

Angel couldn't hear what was being said, but Duncan Millhouse clearly wanted the man to leave. The policeman stuck his head through the curtains.

Angel and the visitor instantly recognized each other.

The policeman's jaw dropped momentarily and his mouth tightened. The man immediately turned round and made for the door. The bell started ringing again. The ringing added a sense of urgency to the situation. In a second the man was gone. The bell stopped ringing.

A red-faced Duncan Millhouse bounced through the curtain into the back room. He was shaking his head. 'People always wanting to sell you things,' he said lamely. 'Er, was there anything else you wanted?'

Angel's eyes shone. 'I thought you wanted to buy. I noticed the signs coming in.'

'We do. We do,' Millhouse replied quickly. 'But the right things, Inspector. Genuine antiques, not rubbish.' He looked briefly back at the closed door.

Angel nodded. He noticed that Millhouse had not even looked at what the man had wanted to sell him. He was considering mentioning this, decided against it, shrugged and turned to leave. He made for the shop door then he turned back.

Duncan Millhouse stretched up to his full height of five feet four inches. 'We know our business, Inspector.'

'I expect you do,' Angel replied with his hand on the door sneck. 'I'll be in touch. Good day to you.' As he closed the shop door, he wondered what business the Millhouses had with Scrap Scudamore, the eldest, the most intelligent and dangerous of the three brothers!

SEVEN

Detective Inspector Angel did not attempt to pick up the trail of Scrap Scudamore as he left the antique shop. The crook would have moved quickly away and dissolved into the crowd of shoppers around the corner once he had left the shop. He lived in a flat in a run-down area of Bromersley. Angel could easily make contact with him anytime he wanted, but he would have relished the opportunity of stopping him to see what he was carrying in that plastic bag.

The inspector made his way to the private car park and pointed the bonnet through the centre of Leeds and on to the open road to Millhouse Hall, which was on his way back to Bromersley.

He was soon at the front door talking to Mrs Moore.

She was in an overall and holding a duster. 'Oh, it's you, Inspector. I thought it might be another newspaper reporter. They're very pushy. They don't take my word for anything. Sir Charles is in London, I'm afraid. He won't be back until Friday.'

'It was your husband I wanted to speak to.'

'Oh, yes?' Mrs Moore replied. Then she opened her mouth wide and applied a hand to her face. 'Is there anything wrong?'

'No. I did say I would need to have a word with him.'

'So you did, Inspector. Come in. I'll get him. He's working in the greenhouses this morning.'

'That's all right. Tell me where he is, and I'll go to him.'

'Just go round the side. That way,' she pointed. 'And on a bit, keeping left, beyond the bushes and you'll see the glass. You can't miss it. He's in one of those greenhouses, or the stables next to them, or round there somewhere.'

Angel was there in a minute. The area was to the side of the Hall, positioned not to obstruct the view of the lake from the house, and behind a screen of trees and bushes created to conceal the incinerator, compost heap, several greenhouses and a stable block.

A man in his sixties, wearing spectacles, overalls, cap and Wellington boots was coming out of the stable block.

Angel called out, 'Mr Moore?'

The man stopped and looked up. He was carrying a plastic container with a wire handle, like a small bucket. He wiped his nose on his sleeve as he approached the policeman. 'Yes, sir. What can I do for you?'

'Detective Inspector Angel from Bromersley CID,' he announced as he picked his way along the track to the outbuildings. 'I would like a few words with you.'

'Oh, yes sir,' he blinked. 'I've been expecting you. Come on in here, out of the wind.'

The gardener turned and led him back into a stable, which housed garden tools, lawnmowers and plastic sacks of fertilizer and weed killer.

'The wife said you'd be wanting to see me.' He put the container down on a bench. 'I was just going to put this rat poison down in the garages. But it can wait.'

Angel pursed his lips. 'Rat poison? Do you get many rats round here?'

'Yes, sir. It's the birdseed and the compost that attracts them. But you've got to be careful of the peacocks and hens, and the ducks and the swans, as well as the wild birds. So I'm very careful with it. I never put it down uncovered. I put it in dry pipes, or I make tunnels with bricks. Birds can't move bricks,' he smiled reassuringly.

Moore pointed to the container he had placed on the bench. 'I reckon there's enough poison in there to kill a thousand birds.'

Angel stroked his chin. 'Or a hundred men?'

'Eh? Maybe. Maybe.' He replied as he adjusted his bottle-bottom spectacles.

Angel glanced round the building. 'I suppose this was a stable at one time?'

'Yes, sir. And along there, there was enough accommodation for eight carriages and twenty-four horses. Now, of course, they're only used for storage and for garaging cars.'

'And how many cars does the family have?'

'Two now. There's Sir Charles's Rolls and Lady Millhouse's Citroen. They had a Mercedes but I think they gave that to Mr Duncan. I've seen him driving around in it.'

'Does Sir Charles drive?'

'Not these days. He enjoys being driven around, and who can blame him, on these busy roads.'

'And did her ladyship drive?'

'Yes. She was a very good driver, considering she came from France, where they drive on the other side of the road.'

Angel smiled. 'Did you see much of her ladyship?'

'No. Not a lot. I'd maybe see her when she came round here for the car, or if she came down here for any veg or flowers for the house. Otherwise hardly at all.'

'Did you get on well with her?'

Mr Moore took off his spectacles and wiped some dust out of an eye. 'Oh yes. She'd smile and wave and call out, "Good morning, Walter." Or something like that. Or she'd come in here, like you are now, if she wanted something for the house. Or if she wanted me to do anything for her.'

His tone changed. He looked closely into the policeman's face. 'She were a nice lady, you know, sir. But my wife is sickened by it all. She knew her a lot better than I did. And she's fed up with reporters continually ringing the bell and on the phone. It's terrible her being murdered like that. And them only been married a few months.'

He replaced the heavy spectacles and with a dirty handkerchief blew his nose. ''Scuse me, sir,' he said, and as he slowly wiped his nose, he peered directly at the inspector and said, 'Have you got anybody for it yet?'

'Not yet. But we will, Mr Moore. Be assured, we will.'

* * *

It was another raw November morning when Detective Inspector Angel arrived at his office. There was a pile of post waiting for him. He ripped the envelopes open roughly to see if there was anything of interest, then threw them, one by one, with a grunt back on the pile on the desk. Then he unfastened the cuff button of his shirt and pulled it and his suit coat sleeve up to the elbow. There was a small square sticking plaster on his arm. From his pocket he pulled out a white packet with pink printing on it. The largest words were 'Nicotine Patch.' He opened the packet, peeled off the backing and slapped it on a bare area of his arm near to an existing patch. He pressed it well on and muttered some words that included an expletive as he quickly pulled down the sleeve and fastened the cuff button.

The phone rang.

'Angel.'

It was the police sergeant on the front desk. 'There's a young lady here. A Miss Melanie Bright, sir. She says you're expecting her. She's Sir Charles Millhouse's chauffeur.'

Angel took a deep breath. 'Oh yes. Get that cadet to bring her down to my office straight away.'

'Right, sir.'

Angel cleared the post off his desk by cramming it into a drawer. He moved round the desk and placed a chair for his visitor just where he wanted it, and a chair by the wall for Cadet Ahaz.

There was a knock at the door.

'Come in.'

It was Ahmed with the blonde chauffeur.

'Miss Bright, sir,' he said.

She stepped into the room uncertainly in black leather shoes with sparkling silver trimming. She was wearing the same light grey suit and white open necked blouse she had been wearing at Millhouse Hall three days ago. It was business-like and yet showed off a tan that Angel thought might have been recently topped up at a high street salon. Her protruding lips, orange lipstick and lip gloss accentuated a natural pout. Her golden hair was drawn back and then lacquered to stick out in different directions at the rear. A few strands dangled down her face. He observed four colours of make up around her eyes. He reckoned she was older than he had originally thought, now that he was closer to her, and in daylight, and was probably about forty. She carried a small black patent leather handbag.

Angel stood up and smiled.

'Please sit down, Miss Bright,' he said indicating the chair positioned to provide him with the best possible scrutiny of every nuance of expression the November light from the window would permit.

'Er, yes,' she said and moved uneasily to the chair.

Ahmed hovered by the door looking attentively at the inspector. Angel nodded to the chair in the corner and the cadet closed the door and took up the position.

Melanie Bright sat on the front part of the chair with her knees together and the handbag on her lap. She was not quite the pushy woman Angel remembered from the brief meeting with her the night he had met her at Millhouse Hall.

The policeman sat down still looking at her.

'Er, thank you,' she said suddenly and quickly. Her voice was froggy and with a strong local accent. Then she asked, 'It's Inspector, isn't it?'

'Yes.'

She coughed. The voice didn't improve. 'Sir Charles said you wanted to see me.'

'Yes. I'm glad you came in. Just a few questions.'

She nodded.

He opened the leather-backed notebook.

'You're Miss Melanie Bright, and you're chauffeur to Sir Charles Millhouse?'

'Yes.'

'Isn't it unusual for a woman to be a chauffeur?'

'Not these days, Inspector.'

He slid a finger up the side of his face, and then down again. She certainly was a good-looking woman. The voice was a letdown. 'Oh, really? And how long have you been in the job?'

'Four years.'

'And what do you actually do? I mean you're not a mechanic or an engineer as well, are you? You don't maintain the car?'

She smiled and shuffled further back into the chair. She looked very attractive when she smiled. 'No. I don't maintain the car. I drive him wherever he wants to go.'

'You drive him to London?'

'Yes. As I said, I drive him anywhere he wants to go. But I come back the same day, usually.'

'Doesn't he drive himself?'

'No. I believe he used to. But it's a pig trying to park in London. It's bad enough taking him to his flat and back.'

'I'm sure. Let me take you back to last Friday. The day Lady Millhouse went missing. What did you do that day?'

'Last Friday? Well, Sir Charles wanted me to pick him up and bring him back home from London as usual. I 'ad to pick 'im up at one o'clock on Marylebone Road, near Regent's Park.'

'Is that where he lives in London?'

'No, Inspector. His flat is in SW1.' She stopped and thought for a moment. 'It was a bit unusual. I don't know why he wanted picking up on the Marylebone Road, but that's what he wanted. I'd have had to collect him from wherever he said.'

'Anyway, I left Bromersley at about nine o'clock. I made good time and I picked him up and got back to the Hall by about five o'clock. The drill is that I gives him a ring on the mobile as I'm getting near, to check whether he's going to be on time or not. I try never to be late. He gets ratty if I'm late. Anyway, he was there, waving his umbrella. And, as I say, I got him home safe.'

'Did he seem in any way different from his usual self?'

She thought before she answered. 'He was a bit quieter than usual. Not at all talkative. I thought he was in one of his moods. He pretended to do some work from his briefcase on the way home, but his mind seemed to be on other things. I watched him, when I could, in the rear mirror. He was a bit strange. I thought he might have been ill. He had been ill, you know. Something he ate, I think. He had been to that posh private hospital near Leeds to see a specialist. I took him a fortnight ago. Anyway, I dropped him off at the front of the Hall with his suitcase. He told me to put the car away and go home. Which I did.'

Angel was particular about the time. 'And this was five o'clock, you said?'

'Yes.'

'Have you a car of your own?'

'Yes,' she replied.

Angel noticed that her forehead was moist and her cheeks red.

'It's hot in here,' she said and she unfastened the top button of her grey suit coat.

It *was* hot in there. Angel wondered if they had turned up the central heating. He pressed on. He tapped the top of his pen on the desktop. 'I have to ask you a very important question.'

Her eyes opened wide. Her eyebrows raised, causing the lines of mascara to arc. 'Yes, Inspector?'

'What time did you get home on that Friday?'

'I came straight home. It would be about five fifteen or so.'

Angel nodded. 'I suppose someone can confirm that?'

Melanie Bright crossed her legs. The light caught her sparkly shoes and twinkled. She considered her reply. 'No. I don't suppose there is anybody. I live by myself, you see.'

He looked her straight in the face. 'A neighbour, maybe?'

She shrugged. The bosom moved. 'Maybe. I dunno. They're a nosey lot round where I live.'

Angel pursed his lips. 'And you stayed home the rest of the evening?'

'Oh no!' she hooted loudly. 'I went out. I always go out on a Friday night. My boyfriend came round after tea and we went out.'

'And where did you go?'

She sat further back in the chair and relaxed her arms. 'There's not a lot of choice in Bromersley, Inspector.' She sniggered. 'We 'ad a few drinks in The Feathers, and then we went to the Can Can Club.' She grinned as she recalled it. 'We had a damn good time.'

'And who did you go out with, Miss Bright?'

'You wouldn't know him, Inspector,' she said with a smile. 'He isn't half a scream!'

Angel sat with his pen poised. 'What's his name, Miss Bright?'

She grinned. 'His real name is Hugo. I call him that. Sounds so posh. But everybody else calls him Scrap Scudamore.'

* * *

There was a knock on the door.

'Come in,' Angel said.

It was DS Gawber. 'Got a minute, sir?'

'Yes. Come in. Have you seen Mac about that carpet?'

'Yes. I've put it in the boot of your car. I thought you'd want to return it, personally.'

Angel was expecting great things from that special piece of carpet. 'Fine. So tell me.'

Ron Gawber shook his head. 'Mac says that no blood nor any other bodily fluids can be recovered to do tests on. The time in the water has seen to that. But he has recovered quite a selection of different human hair. He can get DNA from that if necessary.'

It was a great disappointment to Angel who ran his hand across his mouth and screwed up his eyes. 'It wouldn't prove anything to have the dead woman's hair on it, after all she lived there. It *would* be useful if we had a suspect. Get Mac to save the samples . . . you never know.' Then he added, 'Have we got the right piece of carpet?'

Gawber said, 'Well, Leeds Ops didn't *search* the Beck. It was just that this one was caught in the reeds by the bank where the body was found.'

'From the description, it certainly sounds like the missing one. I'll have a word with the housekeeper, Mrs Moore again. It'll be a good excuse to go up there. Has it been cleaned and dried out?'

'Yes, sir. It's like new.'

'Good. Is there anything else?'

'Yes, sir. It's that funeral tomorrow.'

'Oh. Is it?'

'The undertaker rang up. It's being held at St Mary's. Eleven thirty.'

'Right. I want you in that van with the smoky windows, with a full can of tape. Best take Ahaz with you. He can man the phone and do any running you may need. You'd better liaise with uniformed division and the traffic wardens. We don't want them sniffing round and drawing attention to you while you're filming. I want a picture of everybody who comes out of the church. Let's hope it's not raining. Go early. You should be able to get a good position at the other side of the road right opposite the gates. You know where I mean?'

'Yes, sir.' The sergeant turned to go.

'Afore you go, I've some interesting information for you. Who do you think is Melanie Bright's boyfriend?'

The sergeant considered the question and then smiled slowly. 'Sir Charles Millhouse?'

'Nope.' Angel leaned forward and said, 'The man who's done more chiselling than Thomas Chippendale.'

'Who's that?'

'Scrap Scudamore.'

Gawber put his head slightly on one side and sighed. 'It's all very puzzling, sir.'

Angel nodded. 'What a mixture. Melanie Bright, who could make page three of "The Tart's Weekly." Her chest is like the buffers on Waterloo Station. And Scrap Scudamore. He's so thick, if he'd any tattoos they'd be spelled wrongly.'

'And yet he's the smartest one of the Scudamore tribe.'

'True. It's hard to put those two together though, isn't it.'

The sergeant nodded.

'What do you make of it so far?'

Ron Gawber rubbed his chin and said, 'Well, as I understand it, Sir Charles Millhouse arrived home at five o'clock on Friday afternoon as usual, expecting to be greeted by his wife, but the house is empty. He looks all over the place for her. She's not there. She turns up three days later in Western Beck, naked and strangled to death. She's not on drugs. She's not on the bottle. There's nothing known. No boyfriends. No motive. It doesn't appear to be Sir Charles; he has neither opportunity nor motive. It could be his son, Duncan, for the family fortune — but he'll get that anyway if he has the patience to wait. Duncan's wife, Susan, for the same reason.

And they are giving each other an alibi. The housekeeper, Mrs Moore, her husband, Walter Moore. I doubt either of them. They're honest, hardworking folk. Then we have this unexpected relationship between Sir Charles's chauffeur, Melanie Bright and Scrap Scudamore.'

'That's about it.' Angel suddenly turned sharply to Sergeant Gawber. 'Did Scenes of Crime do a thorough search of the interiors and tailgates of the Rolls, the Citroen and the son's Mercedes? That body had to be transported by some vehicle to Western Beck.'

'Yes, sir.'

'We need a positive match against that carpet. Have Forensic got sample fibres?'

'Yes, sir. They promised their written report by this afternoon. Young Duncan Millhouse protested vigorously at having his car swept. Civil liberties and all that guff.'

Angel ignored the sergeant's news. His mind was on other things. 'Funny thing, her clothes haven't turned up. And her watch, rings and her pearls.'

Gawber ran his hand through his hair. 'We went through all the rubbish bins on the Millhouse estate. We raked through the ashes of the fire down by the gardener's compost heap. Nothing.'

'You didn't look in the lake?'

'Have you seen the size of it, sir?'

'I don't expect we'll ever see anything of them again,' Angel said thoughtfully. And then his face brightened. 'Pearls,' he muttered as he ran his hand across his chin. 'The number of times jewellery turns up in a shop or in an auction after a murder. It's a mark of the intelligence of the murderer. I wonder what will happen this time.'

'How's that, sir?'

'Elementary psychology, Ron. A murderer doesn't want to get caught, does he? Murder is life in prison. An intelligent murderer isn't going to risk being caught trying to make an easy, but relatively paltry, few hundred quid selling his victim's jewellery. The enormity of the risk is obvious. Now a less intelligent murderer might just decide a few extra quid worth taking the risk for.'

He continued, 'Well, we will have to wait and see. It'll be a bonus if they do turn up. But conditions have altered. Drugs have changed the priorities and thinking of crime patterns. The public, especially the younger population, are more stupidly brave when they're filled to the gills with heroin.' Angel shook his head and looked down at the brown linoleum. 'And you should hear some of the latest theories to come out of Hendon!'

Gawber smiled. He had read some of the reports. There was a short pause.

The sergeant said, 'I reckon they'll be buried miles from here.'

Angel didn't hear him. He was staring blankly at the ceiling but he didn't notice the fresh cobweb stretching across from a chain holding the fluorescent tube to the shade, nor the dark mark immediately above the light source.

'Has your wife any pearls, Ron?'

Gawber blinked, then he said, 'She did have, sir. They broke. For no reason. There were pearls all over the house for months. Kept turning up. Under the bed, between the sheets. There was even one in my slipper.'

'Yes,' he said slowly. 'That happened to my wife. Months after the string broke we had a holiday in Scotland. Do you know we took one of the little devils all the way round Argyllshire. It was still at the bottom of the suitcase when we got home.'

'Why, sir? Are you thinking of buying your wife another string?'

Angel smiled broadly. 'Who me? Don't be daft, Sergeant.' He laughed. 'They're a waste of money. I mean what can you do with a string of pearls that break as soon as you look at them?' He shook his head. 'No. No. Just an idea, that's all.' Then he said quickly, 'I'll tell you what, I want you to find out if old Annie Potts still stands the market. She sells all sorts of cheap jewellery. You know who I mean, don't you? Her son was done for possession of cannabis.'

'Yes. You got him off with a caution. I remember.' Then Gawber observed with a smile. '*She* sells pearls.'

'What a coincidence!' Angel grinned. 'And see what you can find out about Hugo Scudamore.'

'Who?'

'Scrap Scudamore to you. What he does for a living these days. Has he any other women besides Melanie Bright in tow. And any other muck you can rake up about him.' Then he added, 'I know he's thicker than newly-weds' gravy, but there might be something interesting.'

'Right, sir.'

'And find out if he owns a car. I'm going out to Millhouse Hall now. Going to have another go at Mrs Moore,' Angel announced, pushing his chair back from the desk. He reached over for his raincoat.

'And ring up Forensic about that carpet. Find out if they have found any trace of anything interesting in any of those cars.'

'Before you go, sir,' Gawber said, running his hand through his hair.

'What?' Angel grunted as he pushed his arm into a sleeve.

'Reporters keep ringing up. They're getting a bit restless, Sir Charles being an MP and all that. Not just the local rag, nationals and editors keep on at me. Even the TV people want an interview. They're all getting a bit fed up with me saying "we are proceeding with our enquiries." They want to speak to you. Can I say that you'll be making a statement or organizing a press conference or something?'

'You can say that we expect to make an arrest shortly.'

Gawber looked puzzled. 'Right, sir.' Then he added thoughtfully, 'And do we, sir?'

Inspector Angel was halfway up the corridor.

EIGHT

Mrs Moore stood in the doorway at Millhouse Hall. 'Oh it's you, Inspector. Did you want to see Sir Charles? I'm afraid he's in London, of course.'

'No Mrs Moore, it is you I want to see,' he said as he strode into the big oak-panelled entrance hall. He patted the roll of carpet he was carrying under his arm.

She stood back from the door to give the policeman easier access.

'Oh, you've brought me carpet back.'

'Not exactly. I just want you to tell me whether this is the piece of carpet that went missing at the same time as Lady Millhouse, that's all.' He partly unrolled the length as far as the floor.

'Oooh yes, Inspector, that's it,' she said wide-eyed and smiling. 'Are you going to put it back where it belongs?'

'I can't leave it, I'm afraid. It's wanted as evidence.' He turned towards the drawing room door. 'Will you show me exactly where it was?'

She closed the front door and ushered him through the nearest doorway. 'Go on through, Inspector.'

The big airy room with its many upholstered chairs, settees, piano, grandfather clock and other furniture looked like a department store showroom without the illumination of the big fire, and the wall lights, the lamps, the chandeliers and people milling around. There was a strong smell of beeswax and glinting brass and silver testified that Mrs Moore had been busy.

She stood at the side of the grandfather clock and waved her hand downwards across the area directly in front of the fireplace. 'There,' she said. 'That's where it was. It's been there for years.'

Angel grunted. 'A sort of hearthrug.'

'Yes,' she said. 'It was.'

He looked at the grandfather clock. He noted that it was secured to the wall by screws through black iron brackets down each side and that the brackets were partly covered by wallpaper. The base of the clock had an arch cut out of the front and the big chintz patterned carpet fitted neatly under the foot all the way back to the skirting board.

A small, satisfied smile appeared on his face. He nodded almost imperceptibly. He listened briefly to the rich sound of the big clock's tick, and then he turned to the housekeeper. 'Very nice. I'll put this carpet down a minute, if you don't mind. There are a few other questions I would like to ask you.'

'If I can help, Inspector,' she said, wiping her sweaty hands on her overall.

He pulled the little leather-backed notepad from his inside coat pocket and turned back a few pages. 'Ah, yes. Lady Yvette used to receive letters from abroad?'

'Yes. From France. I have sometimes picked the letters up from the mat and put them on the hall table. It depended what time the postman delivered. Sometimes I noticed that there was a letter for her with a foreign stamp on it. Yes.'

'Who was it from?'

'Ooooh, I have no idea, Inspector. She wouldn't tell *me*.'

Angel looked into her watery blue eyes then he said, 'Sir Charles and I looked in the bureau for a letter or an address, but there was no indication as to who it might have been. No letters and no addresses. Can you help me?'

'I'm sorry, Inspector. I don't know anything about it. She did seem to be a bit secretive about her post. I mean, she was quick to pick her letters up and disappear somewhere to read them. Especially that one with the Paris mark.'

Angel pursed his lips. 'Would you say it was a man's handwriting, or a woman's?'

'I really have no idea. I didn't examine them.'

'No, of course not.' He looked away, tapped his notebook with his pen thoughtfully and then said, 'Well, if you cannot help me, Mrs Moore, it will remain a mystery forever.'

'I'm sorry.'

'That's all right. Just one more question. You said when you left the house on Friday last, the day her ladyship went missing, that she was wearing a thick woollen red jumper, blue jeans, brown leather shoes, a square-faced wristwatch and a choker of creamy coloured pearls.'

'Yes. That's right.'

'Tell me about the pearls. Did she wear them often?'

'I can't remember ever seeing her without them,' she replied firmly. 'She was very fond of them. Of course, she's only been here through a summer. She may not have worn them in winter.'

'Quite. Can you describe them for me?'

Mrs Moore's jaw dropped. 'Well, what is there to say, Inspector? It was a choker of pearls.'

'Well, how big were the individual pearls?'

'Oh. Not very big.'

'Were they different sizes?'

She nodded. 'The largest about as big as a pea and then getting smaller. They were perfectly round.'

'So how many individual pearls would there be?'

'I don't know.'

'Well, would there be a hundred?'

Mrs Moore licked her lips as she considered her answer. 'Maybe.' Then after a second, she added, 'Perhaps a hundred. Maybe more. I never counted them.'

'Of course you didn't, but there were a lot, weren't there? So they must have been small.'

'I suppose you would say that. Yes. They were small.'

'I just wanted a rough idea so that we know what we're looking for. And what was that colour again?'

'They were that warm, creamy colour. They were very nice.'

Angel carefully wrote it down, made a deliberate full stop, closed the notebook, looked up and smiled. 'That's it for now, Mrs Moore. And thank you.'

He picked up the carpet.

Mrs Moore smiled, then put her hand to her face. 'Oh, and I never even asked you to have a cup of tea.'

'Some other time, perhaps.' He made for the door. 'Goodbye.'

'Goodbye, Inspector.'

He went through the doorway, on to the frontage, past the pillars and down the stone steps on to the gravel at the front of the house. He kicked the gravel noisily as he made his way back to his car. He opened the boot and deposited the roll of carpet into the back. His mobile phone rang. He pulled it out of his pocket.

'Yes.'

'That you, sir?' It was DS Gawber.

'Yes, Ron. What is it?'

'Forensic have found no trace of carpet fibres in the Rolls, Citroen or Mercedes. In fact, they've found nothing of interest to us in any of the cars.'

'Right,' Angel grunted.

'Does that take them out of the frame, sir?'

'Not necessarily. What did you find out about Scrap Scudamore?'

'Not much. Yes. He has a car. An old Jaguar. I've got the number. And he's unemployed. That's all I've got at the moment on him.'

'Right. Shove the car licence number through computer. See what it throws up.'

'I already have done, sir. It's owned by him and a finance company.'

Angel smirked. 'Right. Find out where he garages it. It'll be in the street, I expect.'

'Yes, sir. Oh, you asked me to find out about old Annie Potts.'

'Yes?'

'I phoned the market inspector. She's standing Bromersley Market today.'

Angel beamed. 'Good. I'll go there straight away, and I'll see you in the office in about an hour.'

'Right, sir.'

Angel drove straight to the town centre and stopped on a yellow line outside the Market Hall. The journey had taken twenty minutes. He put the card with the word 'Police' printed on it in the windscreen and made his way through one of six entrances into the modern, concrete building among people, shoppers, lookers, and stallholders shouting out incomprehensible phrases. The interesting smells of ground coffee and freshly baked bread invaded his nostrils. Bromersley Market had a long-standing reputation for good value and big choice, and crowds came in from every village for miles around on market day.

He shuffled through the shoppers in the covered area and out through another entrance to the outdoor stalls. He looked up and down the dozens of stallholders selling everything from fruit and vegetables to bolts of cloth and second-hand pushchairs. Eventually he saw Annie Potts. She was next to a stall selling women's dresses that were hanging from coat hangers protruding in all directions.

Annie Potts was a small, round, elderly woman swathed in coats, scarves and a battered velvet hat. She had a leather apron with a pouch sewn into it, tied around her waist, and she was wearing navy blue mittens. Her face was red, the result of forty years working outside markets in all weathers. She was standing behind a small glass topped showcase in the middle of a spread of brightly coloured jewellery pinned to a piece of curtain material. People with plastic shopping bags were pushing past her stall, mostly not seeming even to give her a glance. She was repinning a brooch to the cloth she was using to display her costume jewellery when she saw the grey raincoat and the big figure of the policeman smiling down at her.

She beamed back and raised her hands. 'Mr Angel! How nice to see you.'

'Hello, Annie. And how are you?'

'I'm all right. What brings you here?'

Without giving him the opportunity to reply, she said, 'Are you following somebody? Can I help you with anything? Oh, I'm glad you came. I was going to get in touch. I was thinking of you only last night. I was in The Feathers. I was having a port and lemon with a friend of mine. A lady.'

She broke off. Angel was being pushed from behind by a lady with a child in a pushchair. She was having difficulty making progress because of people passing the front of the stall in the opposite direction. Three youths pushed past eating fish and chips out of newspaper. The pushchair wheel scrubbed against the bottom of his trouser leg. He leaned over the front of the stall to give them all more room.

Annie Potts continued. 'You know I'll always be ever so grateful to you for speaking up for my son when he got in with that bad crowd. Do you know what he's doing now? He got that job with the bus company. Well you know that, 'cos you helped to get him the interview and gave him a reference. I'll always be grateful to you for that. Well, he got that job as a driver, now he's an instructor. Yes, he teaches other men to drive them big buses round town and all over. Sometimes he has to drive to Manchester. The other week he was taking a party to London. It's a long way to London, isn't it, Mr Angel? And do you know, he's courting! Yes, after all this time. Mind you, she's been married before. I don't mind that. She's a widow with a youngster but she's ever so nice; and she's good for him. Yes. Anyway, I'm sure you don't want to know about me and my lad. As I was saying, I was in The Feathers, me and Edie Longstaff — but you won't know her — last night. And just across from us, two men were talking about that murder up at the big house. Lady Millhouse, I mean.'

A young woman in a headscarf shuffled up next to Angel and was fingering a brooch pinned to the curtain.

Annie turned to her briefly. 'Everything on there is fifty pence, luv. If you want to try it on—'

The young woman scuttled away.

'And *your* name came up.' Annie continued as if she'd never been interrupted. 'One of the men said that he'd heard that you was in charge of the case. The big man said that you'd never find out who'd done it 'cos you 'ad a head as big as a bucket. Them's his exact words. I wanted to say something to him, but Edie Longstaff stopped me. She said it could be dangerous. Well, he was a big lump, and we shouldn't have been listening. Mind you, they were talking that loud we couldn't help but hear them. Any road up, the big one then said that she 'ad a string of fancy men as long as your arm. The other one said that she didn't have any fancy men at all and that *he* ought to know. The big one kept saying that she was only after the money. The smaller chap said that she wasn't. They were getting a bit hot under the collar by this time and they'd had a few drinks. I thought they were going to finish up fighting. But 'ere's the interesting bit, Mr Angel. Do you know who they were?'

The inspector shook his head.

She indicated that he should come closer, and then she said quietly into his ear, 'One was Duncan Millhouse and the other was the eldest of that horrible Scudamore family. They call him Scrap Scudamore. A daft name, if you ask me.'

Angel straightened up. The smile left his face.

Annie Potts nodded and then winked.

The policeman weighed the information carefully before he spoke.

'Well, thank you for telling me, Annie.'

'I think he could be very dangerous, Mr Angel. I know you policemen are specially trained and all that, but you will be careful won't you? I mean I wouldn't want anything like what happened to Lady Millhouse to happen to anyone I know.'

'Don't you worry about it.'

She beamed and nodded. There was a bright twinkle in those old eyes.

'Well now, Annie—' he began.

'Dearie me, I've done all the talking and I haven't asked you what it is you've come for.'

He smiled again. 'That's all right, Annie. I'll tell you. What I want is a nice string of small pearls, that are a warm, creamy colour. Have you got any?'

'Course I have,' she said and she bent down and produced a bunch of twenty or thirty strings from under the stall. They were fastened together by a twist of wire. They were different lengths, colours and sizes. 'Do you want real ones? Or cultured? Or costume?'

Angel began shuffling through the strings. 'Why? What's the difference?'

'About a hundred pounds,' she said with a laugh.

He selected a double string of small, creamy, graduated pearls. 'These look like just what I want.'

'There's some bigger ones here. They're better.'

'These will do fine, Annie.'

'Are you sure? Give 'em here then. I'll put them in a nice box for Mrs Angel.'

'No need Annie, thank you. They'll be fine.'

She saw him look at the paper price ticket stuck on the catch. On it was scrawled ten pounds. He quickly pushed the string of pearls into his raincoat pocket and then pulled out his wallet.

'No, no,' she said. 'Have these on me. As a thank you.'

'No, Annie,' he said taking out a twenty-pound note. 'And I don't want any change.' He thrust it into her hand.

'No,' she protested firmly, and began ferreting in the leather pouch tied round her middle. 'Here, just a minute, Mr Angel.'

He would have none of it. 'Must dash. Take care of yourself, Annie.'

Annie's jaw dropped as she slowly unfolded the note.

'And you watch out, Mr Angel,' she called out after him.

He turned and waved.

She waved back. Then he disappeared into the crowd. She looked at the money, smiled and put the note into the purse inside the leather pouch. Then she looked round for any customers.

Angel dissolved into the crowd and soon reached his car. He pointed it towards the police station. It was only a few minutes away. Although it had been a delight to see Annie Potts and her bright smile, nevertheless his mood was dark. It was worrying to hear further stories of Scrap Scudamore's involvement with Duncan Millhouse. As long as Scudamore was free on the streets, there was a threatening outlook for the town of Bromersley. The quicker he could get Scudamore behind bars, the safer it would be for the community. He needed only one opportunity, one piece of hard evidence and he would have him put away for a long time. Perhaps it was time he had a word with that young man. He was still thinking along those lines when he arrived at the station.

He went into his office and summoned Cadet Ahmed Ahaz to find Detective Sergeant Gawber.

When the trio were sat drinking tea, Angel told Ron Gawber about the conversation Annie Potts had overheard in The Feathers the previous night.

'Isn't it surprising that all our enquiries always seem to lead back to Scrap Scudamore, sir?'

Angel nodded and slowly passed his hand across his mouth. Then he said, 'He's a bad lot, Ron.'

'He could be responsible for Lady Millhouse's murder?'

'It has to be a possibility. I mean we have to ask ourselves what sort of person would commit such a crime?'

'Well sir, what sort of person would commit such a crime?'

Angel screwed up his face as he began to answer the question. 'To answer that we have to get inside the mind of the murderer. To do that we need to find his motive, and we haven't got a motive for Scudamore.'

'Robbery?'

Angel pursed his lips then stretched out his arms, put them at the back of his neck and leaned back in the chair. 'We *do* have a motive for Duncan Millhouse.'

'Oh? What's that then, sir? His inheritance?'

'He might be thinking his inheritance is at stake while Lady Yvette was around. Get her out of the way and the whole pot of gold will eventually come to him.'

Gawber nodded. 'And Susan Millhouse might be very expensive to keep.'

Angel licked his lips and sighed. 'You know, it's times like these I could eat a cigarette.'

Ahmed piped up from the chair by the wall. 'Would you like me to go out and fetch you a packet, sir?'

'No, lad. I've got to fight it. I don't know why. Doctor's orders.'

There was a pause, then Angel said, 'If it was Duncan Millhouse, then his wife, Susan, would know about it, after all she's the one providing the alibi.'

'Money is a strong motive, sir.'

'It *is* a strong motive.' Angel agreed. He arched his back and stretched his arms. 'But there's one that's stronger.'

'Passion.'

'Exactly. Passion!' Then he brought his arms down and bounced them heavily on the desk. 'You asked me what sort of person could commit this crime. I'll tell you. Sir Charles Millhouse. I reckon he could be cool enough to carry it through. He's the sort of man that could commit murder. He's mature enough. He has brains. If it were he, he would be thinking how he could get away with it. His paramount thought would be how not to get caught. His whole being would be geared to covering his tracks. There would be nothing more important to him than to get away with this crime. He wouldn't want to spend the rest of his life swilling out the lavs in Strangeways. He would not be casual about any detail. His mind would be wholly concentrated on this most important matter. It would require immense attention to detail. He would be trying to get into *our* minds too. Yes. Now there's a thought. Him trying to get into *our* minds.'

Gawber smiled wryly.

Angel continued. 'He would be spinning a web of deception that he would hope we would never be able to cut through. It would be good. Not good enough. *Never* good enough. But it would be good.'

The inspector drummed his fingers on the desktop. 'He may have committed murder before and got away with it. His first wife, maybe. I don't think so. The doctor's report was very clear-cut. She died from natural causes. But if Charles *had* committed murder before and got away with it, that would give him tremendous confidence in himself. He'd know how to act the part. He'd be *au fait* with what to expect. He'd know the pressures. He'd know what he'd be subjected to — by the medics, by Forensic and by us. He'd be sweeping up clues and patching up holes as he went along, removing any indication that would point us in his direction. I've said all that on the basis that he could have committed the murder in a fit of rage or passion. Of course a premeditated murder would be much easier to conceal. A highly skilled player would plan it like a military operation. Choose his ground. Choose the time. Arrange an alibi. Provide us with an alternative suspect and then help inveigle the poor sucker. He would leave nothing to chance and therefore would expect to get away with it. He might live on his nerves. It could become a game to him. He might even enjoy playing with us. It could give him a thrill. He would be laughing every time we went down the wrong track. He might even enjoy a perverted thrill of danger whenever we made a move towards discovering his guilt.'

Angel looked across at Ron Gawber. 'It reminds me of a case history I was reading about the other day. It was about an Australian stage hypnotist in the sixties called Harry Harpo. He used hypnotism to commit murder. He travelled the outback with an aborigine guide, doing his act anywhere the white man would pay to watch him. He tried hypnotizing animals, and it seemed to work too. Except for a contrary crocodile that couldn't count up to three. Apparently Harpo thought he had it under the influence but it woke up and took his leg off. So he emigrated to America and had an artificial leg fitted. He married a Milwaukee chiropodist. But they didn't get on. His wife took on a fancy man. Harpo found out about this. He had a radio transmitter fitted inside his leg. It had a loop tape recorder sending his wife a repeated recorded message to a miniature receiver he had had implanted in her ear when he had her hypnotized one time. It was urging her, repeatedly, to kill the man by putting the strychnine he had put in her handbag, into his whisky.'

'And did it work, sir? Was she hypnotized?'

'No, it didn't work. And yes, she was hypnotized.'

'What happened then?'

'Harpo died from strychnine poison. She put the poison into *his* whisky!'

Gawber stared at the inspector intently.

'I only mentioned that case to show you how devious some murderers can be. Also how far wrong their plans can go.'

'And do you think Sir Charles Millhouse is that devious, sir?'

'I'm not sure. But if he was, what's his motive? From all accounts Sir Charles and Lady Yvette were blissfully happy. We have no evidence to say that they weren't. I don't even know whether this was a premeditated crime or not. We have not been able to find out if anyone visited the house between the hours of four and five on that Friday afternoon. That is, between Mr and Mrs Moore leaving, and Sir Charles arriving.'

'Do you mean Scrap Scudamore? With the objective of robbing the place?'

Angel cocked his head to one side. 'Could be. Did he go there to burgle the place and got caught in the act, and had to silence Yvette Millhouse?'

'Then afterwards loaded the body into his car and took it up to Western Beck and dumped it?' Gawber asked.

'It could be like that. Mac said that the body had been on its stomach for a few hours before being dumped in the water. So he may have gone home and waited until the middle of the night. It would have been safer.'

'Would he have needed an accomplice?'

'He could have carried her easily. I think her weight was down at eight stones.'

'Yes, but he'd be under pressure.'

'That's true. She had to be undressed . . . those pearls removed from round her neck. They wouldn't go over her head. They'd have to be unfastened. A little fiddly catch at the back of the neck, the pressure of time, the risk that someone may arrive at any second. Sir Charles could arrive back from London. Would Scudamore's hands be steady enough, would he have the patience to unfasten a tiny catch in such circumstances? Have you seen the size of his hands? He had just throttled the woman. He needs to get out of there — fast. He's unlikely to be in complete control of himself. Would he fiddle with the catch or would he simply yank it free? Would the choker have already been broken in the execution of the murder? Damn it, we all know the thread breaks easily enough! Either way there would be pearls all over the place, wouldn't there?'

Gawber smiled. 'There you go again. Pearls. You're up to something, aren't you, sir? And it's to do with pearls.'

Angel smiled back at him. He shook his head but there was a twinkle in his eye. He went on. 'Then there's all that struggling with arms and elbows and her head to get that jumper off.'

'She didn't *have* to be undressed there.'

'I think she did,' he replied promptly. 'Who would murder her, roll her body into a carpet, put it in a car, drive it somewhere else, unload it, undress it, roll it back in the carpet again, reload it and then later take it up to Western Beck to dump it? Too messy. Take too long. Too risky.'

Ron Gawber nodded. 'You're right, sir.'

Angel looked at him strangely. 'Am I, Ron? Am I?' He shook his head. He looked weary. 'This murderer is harder to find than Harry Houdini's rabbit!'

NINE

The church funeral service for Lady Yvette Millhouse ended. The tuneless wail of the organ could be heard as the chief mourners, Sir Charles Millhouse, Duncan Millhouse and his wife Susan Millhouse, and Mr and Mrs Moore followed the coffin out of the grimy, weather-beaten stone church in the centre of Bromersley. The wind blew the priest's cassock in all directions. Only the colours of the wreaths and flower sprays brightened the scene on that dull November day. The party stood in silence on the pavement as the coffin was put in the hearse.

A blue transit van was parked directly opposite the church gate on the other side of the road. It had a dark glass window in the side. DI Angel hardly gave it a glance as he came out of the church amidst a large crowd of mourners. His interest was purely professional. He expected the murderer to be among the congregation and he was looking for a familiar face. He glanced discreetly to his left and to his right as he shuffled down the steps. As he neared the church gate, he dropped the printed service sheet to give him an excuse to bend down. As he rose back up, he turned round to look back at the hundred or so expressionless faces. He saw what he expected to see: He saw the tall, athletic figure of a man. The man was looking sideways. Angel knew the profile. It was the rough, red face of Scrap Scudamore, who was looking across the mass of bobbing heads at a woman with a pile of blonde hair and an orange suntan. The woman was Melanie Bright. Angel saw her turn towards him. He saw their eyes meet followed by the exchange of small nods and the slightest smile. The man then turned towards the church gates. His eyes may have caught Angel's. The inspector looked away. He pursed his lips. He might have been pleased with his observations but he was not.

The hearse and the two official mourners' cars drove off.

A slim woman all in black with a small veil and very high-heeled shoes hurriedly got into a local taxi, which had just arrived. It had a noisy exhaust and sped off in a cloud of black smoke behind the official cortege. Angel glanced after it.

The inspector decided it was not necessary for him to go to the crematorium, but he would attend the reception at The Feathers. He strolled down the street to the town square and along Bradford Road to the large hotel with a big car park on three sides of it. It was The Feathers. It was the nicest hotel in Bromersley, with choice of three sizes of reception rooms, two bars and offered a dozen or so comfortable bedrooms. A lot of other mourners and sightseers had had the same idea as he had, and he soon found himself being jostled in a queue at the bar. Eventually he was served and he struggled through the crush with a glass of Bromersley Bitter and went into a quiet corner. At the end of the big entrance hall he noticed a sign outside the door of one of the reception rooms. It read: 'Sir Charles Millhouse Reception'.

He put the glass down on a three-legged iron round table. He took out his mobile and dialled. 'Ron . . . Have you finished? . . . Everything all right? . . . Good. I'm at The Feathers . . . Send Cadet Ahaz back to the station and join me . . . Right.'

Five minutes later, DS Gawber came through the door. Angel went over to him, nodded and then went to the bar for a glass of the local brew for him. The crush had gone and the bar was neglected. The barman took his order and then said, 'Hello, Inspector. Don't see you in here often.'

'At your prices is there any wonder?' he said as he picked up his change. 'You must be rich enough to buy a footballer's leg.'

The barman grinned.

Angel and Gawber sat in the corner and waited for the arrival of the funeral party. It didn't take long.

There was a flurry of noise, as the front double doors swung open and four photographers and two men with microphones and tape recorders burst in. They were closely followed by the hotel manager in a dickie bow and morning suit, who was leading Sir Charles and the funeral party to the reception room. At the door, he held the clamouring press men back by holding out his arm and saying, 'Thank you, gentlemen. Thank you.'

Sir Charles looked flustered at the presence of the media. He moved swiftly into the reception room, leaving cries for, 'A statement,' and 'Will you look this way, Sir,' behind him. The reporters stopped at the room door. They lowered their cameras and microphones and immediately crowded around the bar.

Sir Charles brushed his suit down with his hands as he strode across the room to a group of easy chairs on a low stage at the far end. His son, Duncan, and daughter-in-law, Susan, accompanied him. Mr and Mrs Moore and Melanie Bright tagged on behind.

Angel looked at Gawber. They stood up and, leaving their empty glasses on the round table, mingled into the queue of people filtering into the big room. The small woman in the smart black coat and veil seen entering a taxi at the church, gently pushed her way under Angel's arm and ahead of him into the room. She seemed a little unsteady in the high heels. Angel watched her. It was hard to judge her age. She had black hair with a touch of grey. She was wearing a large black hat with a veil that covered her eyes. She was carrying a small black handbag and black kid gloves in one hand and a glass of amber coloured liquid in the other.

Angel nudged Gawber and grunted, 'Who's that?'

'Don't know, sir. I saw her come out of the church.'

The woman manoeuvred her way to a position by a table with four chairs around it, but she didn't sit down.

A waiter was standing behind a table at the far end of the room pouring coffee. Next to him, along the length of the room, were tables covered with starched white tablecloths on which plates, cutlery, red napkins, smoked salmon, pork pies, sausage rolls, salads, trifles, cakes and the like were temptingly displayed.

Sir Charles and the family had glasses in their hands and were seated at the far end of the room. Angel watched them discreetly. They spoke very little. Sir Charles silent and staring blankly out of the window was sipping from his glass now and again. Occasionally, Susan's lips would move a little, then Duncan seemed to offer a very short reply. None of them were interested in the buffet.

Mr and Mrs Moore hovered tentatively near the table where the waiter was serving coffee. Melanie Bright joined them. A few other guests began slowly to drift towards the buffet.

The slim woman in the veil stood on her own, speaking to no one. She still had the glass in her hand. It was empty and she looked round for somewhere to leave it. A waiter with a tray came along and conveniently solved the problem. As she put the glass on the tray, Angel noticed that her hand was expensively manicured and that she was not wearing any rings. An important choker of pearls fitted closely around her brown, suntanned neck. His eyes lingered on the jewellery. He thought of Yvette Millhouse's pearls.

A man in a sleek suit approached Sir Charles. The MP put his half full glass on a table beside him and stood up. The two men shook hands and began talking animatedly. Two more people went across to the family and then another couple. A small crowd began slowly to gather around Sir Charles and the family.

Several guests were lighting up cigarettes. Angel sniffed and glared at them.

The woman in the veil began to walk slowly, a yard at a time, along the edge of the spongy maroon carpet towards the family. She was now wearing black gloves and carrying the handbag well up her arm. She stopped, looked back to see if anyone was observing her. Angel looked away. She didn't notice him. Then he saw her making more progress towards the small group. Angel's eyes followed her every move. He nudged Ron Gawber and whispered urgently, 'Watch that woman.' He nodded towards her. 'Don't take your eyes off her.'

She continued her slow advance towards the group of family and friends. She increased her pace. Gawber sensed the urgency. He moved closer towards her. He glided past the buffet table. Angel went the other route by the door entrance and the long wall with people seated on chairs, his eyes constantly on her. She didn't look back. She had her target in view. She was a yard behind Sir Charles. His half full glass was on the table only two feet from his hand.

She reached out and passed her closed gloved hand over the rim of the glass, opened it, then withdrew her hand and glided away at speed.

Angel saw it. So did Gawber. The woman passed swiftly behind the group and back into the body of the guests. The inspector said, 'Get her. Don't let her go.' Gawber rushed off.

Angel turned to Sir Charles, who had picked up the glass and was about to take a sip.

Angel knocked his wrist. 'Excuse me, sir.'

The glass fell to the floor.

Sir Charles turned round angrily. 'What on earth do you think you're doing?'

'Very sorry, sir.'

'What the hell is going on, Inspector?'

'May I speak to you privately?'

'What is it?' he replied testily. 'Look at my glass!'

The glass had landed unbroken on its side on the carpet. Angel swiftly pulled out a handkerchief, turned the glass upright and picked it up by its foot. It was empty of wine but was still wet and contained sediment.

Sir Charles eased away from the crowd and leaned over to the policeman.

'I saw someone — a woman — drop something in your glass. I had to stop you drinking it,' Angel said quietly.

Sir Charles's jaw dropped. His eyes shone. He stared at the glass in Angel's hand. He said nothing. He picked his way back to his chair and sank into it. He put the back of his hand to his mouth.

Duncan had seen the glass fall to the floor. He looked down at the stain on the carpet and then at the glass in Angel's hand. 'Are you all right, Dad?'

Susan leaned over the chair and pulled the cigarette out of her mouth. 'What's the matter?'

'I should get him a brandy. He's had a shock,' Angel said quietly.

'Dad. Dad!'

Sir Charles said nothing and looked straight ahead.

A waiter appeared. 'Is everything all right, sir?' he said to Duncan Millhouse.

'A double brandy, quickly please.'

'At once, sir.' The waiter rushed off.

The crowd did not notice what had happened. The buzz of conversation continued uninterrupted.

* * *

Angel strode down the green corridor to the CID room. He was carrying a paper bag, carefully holding it in front of him in both hands. The door was open and several officers were seated at computers. Cadet Ahmed Ahaz was nearest the door. He saw Angel and promptly stood up.

'Yes, sir?' he said smartly.

'Where's DS Gawber?'

'I don't know, sir. But I will look for him for you, if you wish it.'

'Do that, Ahmed. Ask him to come to my office pronto.'

'I will sir. Pronto, sir,' he said and smiled showing his white, even teeth.

Angel turned and went along the corridor to his own office. He placed the paper bag on the desk, put his raincoat on the coat stand and then peeled off his suit coat. He undid his shirtsleeve and rolled it up to reveal a flesh-coloured sticking plaster on his arm. He pressed it down with his fingers and grunted angrily. Then he opened a drawer in the desk and shuffled around the front of it. Eventually he found what he was looking for: a white paper packet labelled 'Nicotine Patches.' He peeled the covering off a patch and slapped it on his arm near to the existing one. He pressed it down firmly, looked at it and muttered, 'Now work, damn you, work!'

He fastened up his shirt cuff and put on his coat. He was adjusting the collar when there was a knock at the door.

'Yes!' he bellowed.

It opened. It was DS Gawber. 'Everything all right, sir?'

'Yes. Come in. How did it go?'

'I got her back to the station.'

'Sit down.'

He pulled the chair across from the wall and sat down. 'I charged her with disturbance of the peace.'

'That's right. We'll want her for attempted murder, but that'll hold her for twenty-four hours. Has she a solicitor?'

'I don't think so, sir. I booked her in, cautioned her and tried to ask her some questions, but she won't say anything.'

'She won't say *anything*?' He grunted. 'What did she say in reply to the charge?'

'She simply said, "I have nothing to say." '

Angel grunted and pursed his lips.

'Anyway she was carrying a passport in her handbag. She is French — a French foreign national. Her name is Simone Lyon. And she's carrying a return ticket to Paris. It has a Paris address on it. That's all I've managed to find out.'

'French is she? And she won't talk? Does she understand English?'

'Oh yes. You should have heard her carry on when I arrested her! She speaks English all right, sir.'

'Where is she now?'

'Number one interview room, sir.'

'On her own?' Angel asked quickly.

'No, sir. There's a WPC with her.'

Angel nodded and drummed his fingers on the desktop. 'Has she been searched?'

'Not yet. I was waiting for you, sir.'

'Right. Move her to a cell. Have her searched. Then fingerprint her. Make sure she's comfortable. Give her a cup of tea or something now, and a meal later on.'

'Then shall I have another go at her?'

'No. Leave her overnight. And tell the WPC not to engage in any kind of conversation. She must be polite, of course. As polite as a dustbin man at Christmas, but no chit-chat. All right?'

Gawber nodded and smiled knowingly. 'Yes, sir. And *you'll* have a go in the morning.'

Angel looked at him and a small smile appeared on his face. 'How well you know me, Ron.' Then he added with a wink, 'And you know what else they say?'

He shook his head. 'No, sir.'

The inspector stood up and leaned over the desk. 'If you want a pig to go down a ginnel, pull its tail!'

Gawber smiled and stood up. 'Oh.' He remembered something. 'Is Sir Charles all right, sir?'

'Yes. He says he doesn't know the woman. Never seen her before. And he's no idea why she would put anything in his glass.'

'Strange.'

'Very strange.' Angel leaned across the desk and picked up the paper bag. 'Here's that glass. It'll have my prints on it, and Sir Charles's. Have Scenes of Crime check it out, record it, then let Doctor Mac have it. Tell him it's urgent. Tell him I think he'll find it contains rat poison.'

'Rat poison, sir?' he exclaimed raising his eyebrows. 'How do you know that?'

'An educated guess, Ron. An educated guess.'

Gawber shook his head and smiled as he picked up the bag. He left quickly and closed the door.

Angel looked after him and sighed. He stared across the desk at the oak grain on the office cupboard in front of him. After a few seconds, he lowered his eyes on to the pile of papers on his desk. His mouth was dry. He licked his lips. He could murder a cigarette. 'I'm as dry as the small print on a mortgage,' he muttered. He picked up one letter after another and slowly turned each one over on to another pile. He was looking at them but not reading them. The contents were not registering. They might just as well have been written in Chinese. They were just words, black on white. It was just babble. He lowered his hands. His eyes returned to the oak cupboard door. He stared at the brown varnished woodwork. The grain on the door went out of focus. A mist appeared. He was daydreaming. He saw the petite French woman, all in black with the hat and the veil, and wearing the pearl choker — those pearls again — and a close up of her hand passing over the top of Sir Charles's glass. Then the look of shock and terror in the MP's eyes. The French woman must be either very stupid or very desperate. If she was desperate, what was she desperate about? It most assuredly was rat poison. It was a very serious offence. It was nothing less than attempted murder. And how did Angel know it was rat poison? He didn't *know*. He couldn't explain. There must be a reason. He had just told DS Gawber it was rat poison. It is as if the brain works things out for itself. Maybe he'll be wrong? Perhaps it won't turn out to be poison at all. Maybe it was a vitamin pill? Perhaps the cow *did* jump over the moon after all?

There was a knocking sound. Somebody was knocking at the door. It brought him out of his reverie with a jolt. The knock was repeated.

'Come in!'

The door opened slowly and Cadet Ahaz was there tentatively carrying a plastic cup. 'Excuse me, sir. I thought you might like a cup of tea.'

Angel smiled.

He sipped the tea and returned to the papers on his desk. He made good progress and remained for several hours with his head in the reports and letters uninterrupted. His concentration was suddenly disturbed by the slam of a door and loud voices along the corridor passing his office. He looked at his watch. It was six o'clock. It was the changeover of the shifts. He was tired. He wanted to get that black funeral tie off. A stiff whisky, a hot meal, and his sheepskin lined soft leather slippers beckoned. He went home.

The following morning he arrived in the office. He had had a peaceful evening at home. He had had to chase off some newspaper reporters who had ambushed him outside the station wanting news of the French woman, Simone Lyon. He had told them that she was helping them with their enquiries, and that at the moment, he could tell them nothing. He had wondered how they had discovered her name until the local reporter for the *Bromersley Herald* told him that she was staying at The Feathers and that she had signed into the hotel in that name. It was an interesting piece of information and he wondered if there would be anything helpful in her luggage. He must get Gawber to take a look at it.

He was preparing himself to interview Simone Lyon when Cadet Ahaz knocked on the door.

'Good morning, sir,' Ahmed said beaming. He had a bunch of letters from the morning's post.

The phone rang.

'Just a minute, lad,' he said to Ahmed as he picked up the phone. 'Angel,' he said into the mouthpiece.

It was Superintendent Harker, the inspector's immediate superior. 'Michael, a triple nine call has just come in. A man has found a male body at the back of the Can Can Club.'

Angel's jaw tightened. 'Yes, sir.'

'The finder has already sent for an ambulance but I want you to get there before it does.'

Angel licked his dry lips. 'On my way, John.'

He slammed down the phone.

'Yes, sir.'

His face grim, he reached out for his coat and turned to Ahmed. 'Find DS Gawber. Tell him a body has been found at the back of the Can Can Club. Tell him to meet me there.'

The boy's jaw dropped. The whites of his big eyes reflected the light. His pulse was racing. He looked down at the back of his hands. The skin had turned to gooseflesh.

'Er, yes sir,' he said mechanically as he watched Angel race out of the office.

It took only five minutes for Angel to reach the Can Can Club. It was situated on one of the secondary roads leading from Bromersley town centre. The building had been a small purpose-built cinema of the nineteen twenties. It had closed down and been for sale for a decade or more before a local businessman had had the enterprise to buy it. He had levelled off the floor, had a few coats of paint thrown at it, and some second-hand tables and chairs brought in from a club in Manchester that had closed down. He had had coloured neon lights installed above the three main doors and he had opened it a year or two ago. It had a food and drinks licence, and a pop singer, comedian or novelty act was engaged from time to time to entertain the townsfolk.

Detective Inspector Angel arrived to discover a police car parked at the side of the building. Its amber light was flashing. A police constable was putting out blue and white tape warning, 'Do Not Cross. Police.'

Angel crossed to the PC. 'What's happening then, lad?'

The young PC lowered the tape. 'I'm glad you've come, sir. I've only just got here. There's a man's body between these dustbins and the skips,' he said panting.

'Have you seen anything of an ambulance?'

'No, sir.'

The PC pointed to the walled off area adjacent to the nightclub in which were six grey dustbins and two rubbish skips. 'He was found a few minutes ago by an old man who lives opposite. He was returning from the newspaper shop with his dog. The dog got interested in something behind the bins and wouldn't respond to his call. He had to come across to get hold of the dog and that's when he saw the body. It's pretty gruesome, sir.'

'Right, lad. You carry on.'

An ambulance arrived.

Angel moved into the area and peered behind the bins and then between the two skips. He saw a rumpled pile of clothes on the wet ground. It had a head at one end and shoes at the other. The eyes were open and looking upwards, one arm lay awkwardly above the head. There were no obvious signs of the cause of death. A brick from a jagged wall end was on the tarmac a yard or so from the dead man's head.

A red-faced ambulance man in a blue and green uniform came running up to Angel. He was carrying a bag.

'Where is he?' he asked urgently.

'I think you're too late, lad.' He pointed down between the two skips.

The ambulance man said nothing. He reached over the body and grabbed the wrist. He held it for a second. Then he touched the neck.

He stood up. 'Aye, he's stone cold. Any idea who it is?'

Angel didn't answer the question. He knew who it was. 'You can leave it to us, lad,' he replied rubbing his chin.

The PC came up. 'He's a goner isn't he?'

The ambulance man looked at the PC and said, 'Aye. I can't do anything for him.' Then he turned to Angel. 'You can have him. I'll be off.'

As the ambulance drove off, three vehicles arrived from different directions. The Scenes of Crime van, Dr Mac the pathologist and DS Gawber.

All three made for Angel.

'Help yourselves, lads,' he said to the Scenes of Crime team nodding towards the bins. They glanced at the body and then returned to the van and began to unpack their special clothing.

The old pathologist looked over his spectacles. 'Oh, it's you, Mick. Good morning to you.' Then he looked down between the skips and back at Angel. He grimaced. 'Messy. Very messy.'

Angel noticed the lace curtains of some of the houses opposite were drawn back and curious faces had appeared at the windows and were staring across at the scene.

'Morning, Mac. If you want privacy, you'll have to put up a tarpaulin,' he said, indicating the houses opposite.

'We'll see how it goes,' he replied looking up and pulling on a white rubber boot. 'We may not have to be here long.'

'Did you have time to look at that wine glass I sent to you yesterday?' Angel asked tentatively.

Dr Mac looked up at him and smiled. 'The one you thought contained rat poison?'

'Yes.'

'I have,' the doctor replied as he tucked his trouser bottoms into the boots.

'And what did you find?'

'Rat poison. Common or garden rat poison, just as you said. You can buy it in any hardware or gardening shop. It's coloured blue to make it unmistakable.'

Angel smiled. 'I know the stuff. Thanks, Mac. Thank you very much. That's a pint I owe you.'

Dr Mac proceeded to pull on the other rubber boot. 'You're welcome. That's practically a whole brewery you owe me.'

Angel stroked his chin. He was in no mood to banter this cold November morning. Eventually he asked, 'Would it kill a man, Doc?'

The pathologist pulled on a white rubber glove. 'If you could get a big enough dose into a man, it would.' The glove snapped tight as he released it. 'It would taste pretty foul, though. The most successful way of polishing someone off would be to disguise the taste in cocoa, drinking chocolate or some patent medicine — anything liquid with a strong flavour — and administer small doses over a period of time.'

'Thanks, Doc.'

'Is that what you wanted to know?'

'That's *exactly* what I wanted to know.'

Doctor Mac nodded and turned towards the rubbish skips.

DS Gawber came up to Angel panting. 'Got your message, sir.'

He told him briefly how the body had been found. 'I want you to get a statement from the man who had been walking his dog. And see what you can find out from the other people in the houses opposite. See if anybody had seen anything unusual last night, during the night or this morning. Or heard any shouting or fighting.'

'Right, sir.'

Angel pointed to the body. 'And see if you can find out his movements over the past twelve hours or more. You know what to do. I can't do anything useful here. I'll get back to the office.'

'Yes, sir.' He glanced in the direction of the rubbish bins. 'Any idea who the murdered man is?'

Angel nodded. 'Oh yes. I know who it is.' The corners of his mouth turned down. 'It's been coming to him for a long time. It's Scrap Scudamore.'

TEN

Angel arrived back at the police station. He went into his office and began preparing himself to interview Simone Lyon. The case against her was more serious now that Dr Mac had confirmed that there was poison in the wine glass. What she might have to say might help with the solving of the murder of Lady Yvette Millhouse. He picked up the phone, dialled a number and instructed the duty jailer to bring her to an interview room. Then he moved swiftly there himself. He switched the tape recorder on to standby and put a new tape in the machine. He looked round the room and noticed a statement form on the seat of a chair. He picked it up, glanced at it, noted the date and then dropped it in a wastepaper basket. He fastened a suit coat button and adjusted his tie. Then he went to the door. A woman's protesting voice indicated that Simone Lyon was on her way.

'Where are you taking me, young man?'

The black suited lady, now without the hat and veil, was walking quickly along the green corridor escorted by a PC.

Angel opened the door wider. 'In here, if you don't mind,' he said pleasantly. He nodded a 'thank you' to the constable who turned round and disappeared round the corner.

She cautiously came into the room, checked off the four chairs, the small table, the high windows, the cream painted walls, the telephone and the red light of the audio recorder. Her big eyes looked up at him.

He looked down at her. She was aged about fifty. Her high cheekbones, blue eyes and thick black hair indicated that she had been very beautiful in her younger days and was not unattractive now. Her face was lined, her eyes tired, her mouth turned down at the corners. She spoke clearly with a rich, deep voice, with a nasal intonation typical of the French. Her pronunciation of consonants was very distinctive.

She looked Angel straight in the face. 'I am not saying anything. I don't care what you do to me.'

'Please sit down. I am not going to do anything to you.'

He sat in the chair nearest the door. She hesitated then slowly sat down opposite him. She stared at him fixedly.

He looked across the table at her, then he turned to the audio recorder and pressed the switch. 'I have to switch this on whether you speak to me or not. I have something to say to you and it is necessary to make a record of it.'

She defiantly changed the direction of her stare to the wall opposite.

Angel spoke towards the microphone rapidly, 'It is ten fifteen on Wednesday morning, November the fifteenth. This is interview room number one. Present are Detective Inspector Angel and Miss Simone Lyon. Miss Lyon was arrested and charged yesterday with disturbing the peace. Confirmation of new evidence has come to light that requires her to be charged with a more serious offence.'

He turned briefly back to her. 'Miss Lyon, I am charging you with the attempted murder of Sir Charles Millhouse. You do not have to say anything but whatever you do say may be recorded and used in evidence against you. Do you understand that? Do you have anything to say?' He looked at her and raised his eyebrows to encourage her to reply. She continued to stare at the blank wall.

He repeated the question. 'Miss Lyon, do you have anything to say?'

She remained silent.

He pursed his lips and said, 'Very well. Miss Lyon refuses to answer. Now I am going to ask Miss Lyon if she has legal representation.'

He stared at her. There was a pause. She remained tight lipped.

'You haven't, have you?' he said, raising his voice slightly.

She shook her head furiously. Then looking at the recorder light, she snapped out a curt, 'No.'

Angel smiled briefly then said, 'Well, do you want legal representation?'

There was silence.

He added, 'I recommend that you employ a solicitor. This is a very serious offence. You could end up in prison for a long period of time.'

'No,' she snapped.

Angel put his elbows on the table and then said quietly, 'The situation is this, Miss Lyon. Detective Sergeant Gawber and I both saw you deposit a substance into Sir Charles Millhouse's wine glass at The Feathers yesterday. I recovered the glass and sent it to the lab for examination. It proved to contain rat poison. If you have nothing to say in your defence, the matter will go to court and you will be accused of attempted murder by poisoning. It seems inevitable that you will be found guilty and, although it is not for me to suggest the sentence, I would think you would be facing a jail term of up to four years.'

He looked straight across the table at her. She was looking at the wall trying to avoid his eyes. He looked at the plain pearl choker enhancing her slender neck and then up to her eyes. It was difficult to calculate what she was thinking. She didn't seem to be afraid. She didn't seem to be stupid either.

'Don't you want to say anything?'

He waited a few seconds and then said, 'Very well.' He turned to the recorder. 'Interview terminated at ten twenty.' Then he picked up the phone and dialled a number. 'Interview room number one. Will you escort the prisoner back to the cells?' He returned the handset to its cradle.

Suddenly Simone Lyon said, 'Inspector, how long do you intend keeping me locked up?'

Angel stood up and looked down at her. 'If you remain silent, then your case will be heard at a preliminary hearing. That could be in a few days' time. Then you will be transferred to a prison awaiting trial. That could take weeks or even months.'

She inhaled quickly. Her mouth tightened and exaggerated the skinny neck.

He made his way to the door and opened it. Then looking back at her he said quietly, 'You would be well advised to see a solicitor, you know.'

A police constable arrived.

She stood up and walked to the door with her nose in the air.

Angel sighed as he looked at her. She was not the usual type of criminal he was used to interviewing. 'Is there anybody you would like me to contact, to tell them you're here? You would almost certainly be allowed to see them.'

She turned back. 'There is nobody.'

He nodded to the police constable who stood back to let her pass in front of him. Angel watched them disappear round the corner and down the corridor. He returned to the recorder, ejected the audiotape, switched off the machine and slowly strolled out of the room.

With his head down and his hands in his pockets, he meandered slowly up the corridor. This case was tiring. He was going nowhere fast. Time was ticking on and he still didn't have any concrete evidence. He didn't believe in luck, but that's what he was hoping for. There were two murders and no clear motive for either. Scudamore's murder could be a disagreement with the local gangland heavies. Little Caesars were frequently marking out their territory and needed to make an example of some little crook muscling in on their ground. It could easily have been a man brought in from Leeds or Manchester to settle an old score.

Lady Yvette's murder was very different. What was the motive?

As he looked down at the stone-coloured tiles, he saw a red and gold cigarette packet. He kicked it forward a few feet, then, as he reached it, he gave it another kick. And another. He remembered his school days and how he used to fly up the wing with the ball never more than a yard from his toecap, apparently tied to his feet by a piece of invisible elastic. All inhibitions gone, he ran up to it and made a further mighty lunge at it towards his office door.

'It's a goal!' he called spontaneously.

'Are you all right, Inspector?' He suddenly heard a woman's voice inquire.

147

He straightened up and looked round. A young police-woman appeared from behind. She had been walking up the corridor. She looked knowingly into his eyes and smiled brightly at him. He looked at her sourly. Then he noted how pretty she was. He tried to smile back and said, 'Er, erm. Some scruffy devil's dropped a cigarette packet.' He pointed to the floor.

'Yes, sir,' she said still smiling.

'I was picking it up,' he explained lamely. He continued watching her.

Without slowing her pace, she maintained that smile at him until she went out of sight round the corner.

He stood there, watching her disappear, then he smiled, reached down and picked up the battered cigarette packet. It was nice to feel it in his hands. It was clearly empty, but nevertheless he found the squashed top, tore it open to see if by some miracle there was a cigarette inside. There wasn't. He pulled a face as he went into his office and closed the door. He tossed the cigarette packet into the wastepaper bin.

He slumped down in the chair and leaned back. He looked up at the cobweb and stretched his arms into the air. He stayed like that for a minute, then suddenly he lowered his arms, leaned forward and opened a drawer in his desk. He pulled out the string of pearls he had bought from Annie Potts on Bromersley market. He dropped them noisily on the desk. He opened another drawer and took out a pair of scissors.

* * *

'Thank you for coming in, Mr Millhouse. Please sit down.' Inspector Angel closed the office door and indicated the chair at the other side of his desk.

Duncan Millhouse unfastened his raincoat and sat down. He said nothing. He was not a happy man. The corners of his mouth were turned down as if there was an unpleasant smell under his nose.

'I also wanted to see your father, but there was no reply from the house.'

'He's gone to London,' he said bluntly.

'I phoned late yesterday afternoon,' Angel explained.

'He went straight from the reception.'

'Yesterday? After the funeral?'

'Yes. His chauffeur, Miss Bright, took him in his car. He's an MP you know. He said that he *had* to be there. There was a big vote coming up.'

Angel's bushy eyebrows went up and then down again quickly. He didn't want Duncan Millhouse to see that he was surprised. He pressed on quickly. 'I'll come straight to the point, Mr Millhouse,' he said evenly.

Duncan Millhouse nodded. 'Good.'

The inspector thought the reply was insolent but he continued not showing his attitude. 'You will have heard that Hugo or Scrap Scudamore has been murdered?'

Duncan swallowed almost imperceptibly. 'Yes.'

'I understand that you were a friend of his?'

'No, I wasn't,' Duncan said quickly. 'I knew him. That's all.'

'You used to have business dealings with him?'

'Well yes. As you know, I used to buy things from him from time to time.'

'What sort of things?'

'Well, er, different things.'

'Like what?'

'Oh, er, things for me to sell.'

'Like stolen things. Like jewellery?'

'Well sometimes jewellery, yes. Not stolen things. No. I wouldn't buy anything stolen. There's nothing stolen in *my* shop.'

'Good.' Angel looked at him closely as he asked, 'He didn't bring any pearls, for instance?'

Duncan looked at him for a second before he answered. 'No. He didn't bring any pearls.'

'What else did Scudamore bring to your shop?'

Duncan Millhouse hesitated. 'Small bits. Like brass or copper. Sometimes he might have brought a painting.'

'And where did he get these small bits from?'

'I don't know. He used to scratch round fleamarkets, I suppose, antiques fairs, Bromersley second-hand market, house clearances. I don't know. I never asked him.' 'How did you decide the price of an item?'

'He asked a price. If I could see a profit in it for me, I would agree.'

'What if you didn't agree?'

'Well, I might suggest a price at a level where I *could* make a profit.'

'And did he usually agree to that?'

'Sometimes. Not always.'

'What happened if you didn't agree?'

'He would have gone away. He would have tried to sell it to another dealer. I tried to buy as much as I could from him so that he would continue to bring me good stuff that I could have sold at a profit.'

'After all this time, you must have had a good relationship with him, I suppose.'

'Well, I wouldn't put it like that. He's not my style, Inspector. It's all very well to *buy* from a man, but you don't have to like him.'

'I thought you *did* like him. I was told that he was a regular drinking pal of yours. You've been seen at The Feathers.'

'Who told you that?' He asked curtly.

'Several people.'

'Several people. What is this? He's *not* in my circle of friends.'

'Who is in your circle of friends?'

'Well, I have to be sociable. And a few pints of lager may well lubricate the wheels of business, if you know what I mean.'

'Oh yes. I know what you mean,' Angel said lingering on the phrase. 'I know what you mean. But you were both heard discussing matters that one would describe as personal to your family. Not the sort of chit-chat you might have with a man you had a business relationship with, that you had met in the pub and was buying a drink for.'

'What do you mean?'

'On one occasion, you were overheard discussing the morals of your stepmother for one thing.'

'Never.'

'You were,' Angel said firmly. 'Goodness knows what else you might have discussed while you were drinking ale.'

Duncan's face reddened. 'I can hold my liquor, Inspector. Anything I might have said to Scrap Scudamore would be to defend any allegation he might have made about Yvette. He was a mean, corrupt man. I only *bought* from him. I didn't share anything else with him, and I certainly would not willingly have discussed my family with him.'

'Very well, sir. I have taken note of that,' Angel said, not very convincingly. Then he asked quietly, 'Where were you last night, after the funeral, between eleven o'clock last night and four o'clock this morning?'

Duncan Millhouse took in a deep breath and looked into the policeman's eyes. 'Well I wasn't outside the back of the

151

Can Can Club, I can tell you that!' He snapped. 'I was at home with Susan, my wife. We were there all evening and all night. We didn't go out. I had just been to my stepmother's funeral. I was not in the best sorts.'

'Quite. And your wife would testify to that, wouldn't she.'

'Yes.'

'And that, of course, gives your wife an alibi for last night also.'

'Yes.'

'Like it does for the time your stepmother was being murdered.'

'Yes.'

Angel had that feeling that he was not going to extract any useful information from this man. It wasn't that he was clever. It was simply that there was nothing new to ask him. All questions produced answers that did not further the investigation. The real problem was that there wasn't enough evidence, and without a motive there wasn't even a case. He had one further question. It might reveal a motive.

'Tell me, Mr Millhouse, how's business?'

'Fine.'

'You're doing well, are you?'

'Well enough.'

Angel pursed his lips before he spoke. 'I thought things had taken a downturn in the antiques trade. I hear the Americans no longer buy the container loads they used to buy. Dealers have stopped coming over in their hordes.'

Duncan forced a smile. He was surprised to hear that Angel knew anything about the antiques business. 'That's right, Inspector. But it doesn't affect me. I sell a lot of stripped pine. There's still a big market for old furniture that has been reclaimed from old houses, you know.'

Angel nodded and stared at him for a few seconds. Unexpectedly, the man was still smiling. It was a forced smile. It stayed frozen on his lips.

* * *

The phone rang.

'Angel.'

It was the station telephone switchboard operator. 'There's a woman called Mrs Hannah Moore on the line, sir. She asked for you. She says she's the housekeeper to Sir Charles Millhouse.'

'Oh yes. Put her through.'

There was a click.

'Good morning, Mrs Moore. Inspector Angel. What can I do for you?'

'Oh Inspector.' The woman's voice wailed. He knew something was wrong. 'Lady Yvette's car has been stolen from the garage. My husband has just come up from the greenhouse to tell me.'

'Any sign of a break in?'

'No. The garage wasn't locked up. It was in a garage behind the greenhouses. I can't get in touch with Sir Charles to let him know. He's not answering his London number. I thought I should report it to somebody.'

'You did right, Mrs Moore. I'll come straightaway.'

He put down the phone. This was the opportunity he had been waiting for. He knew exactly what he was going to do. He opened a desk drawer and pulled out a small plastic bag. It was bursting with loose pearls from the necklace he had taken to pieces the day before. He selected several pearls and looked at them gleaming in the palm of his hand. He nodded approvingly. They looked valuable but were worth very little.

He carefully put them into his pocket and returned the bag of pearls to the desk drawer and closed it.

Ten minutes later he was stumping through the gravel at the front of Millhouse Hall. Mrs Moore appeared at the big door under the portico. The alarm buzzers and the noise of the car on the gravel would have indicated his arrival.

'Ooooh, come on in, Inspector. And this time you'll have a cup of tea,' she said with a determined nod of the head.

He climbed the stone steps and followed her into the house.

She closed the door and showed him into the drawing room. 'Sit yourself down, Inspector. I am on my own. My husband is working in the greenhouses. We'll go down there in a minute. I'll just make that tea, or would you rather have coffee?'

'Tea's fine thank you, Mrs Moore.'

She sailed out into the hall.

Inspector Angel listened to the rapid clickety-click of her shoes on the parquet flooring of the entrance hall. When he was satisfied she was well into the kitchen, he rose to his feet. This was the opportunity he had been waiting for. He dug into his pocket and pulled out the pearls. He selected one and approached the grandfather clock. He knelt down on the thick maroon carpet and carefully pushed it through the cutaway of the clock foot. With one finger, he pushed the pearl through the opening and round to one side. Then he returned to his feet, stood back and surveyed the clock from different angles to make sure it was not visible. He nodded with satisfaction.

A clickety-click of shoes heralded the imminent return of the housekeeper.

Angel was comfortably back in the chair when Mrs Moore entered the room with a tray of tea and a plate of biscuits.

'There you are,' she said lowering the tray on to a wine table strategically placed by his chair.

Angel smiled at her. 'Thank you. Now tell me about the car,' he said picking up the cup and saucer.

'Yes. Well my husband went down to the greenhouses at nine o'clock and was clearing out some tomato plants, I think. He wanted something from the garage and noticed the door was open and swinging. He went to see why it was loose and discovered that the Citroen was gone.'

'How did the thief gain access?'

'The door is never locked.'

'Where is the car key?'

'Her ladyship would have had that.'

Angel recalled that Yvette Millhouse's handbag had not been found. 'Was there a spare key?'

'I don't know. I never saw it. Perhaps Sir Charles will know.'

'And you say you cannot reach him by phone?'

'I have his London flat number. I have tried to reach him several times. He must be in the House or at a meeting.'

Angel sighed. He returned the cup to the tray. 'I have the car licence number. I'll put out a nationwide search for it,' he said as he made for the door.

'I'll take you down to the garage, Inspector.'

'There's no need. You've given me all the information I need.'

The housekeeper's jaw dropped slightly.

He turned back. 'Oh, Mrs Moore.'

'Yes, Inspector?'

'Did you know a man called Hugo or Scrap Scudamore? Has he been to this house, as far as you know?'

She put her hand to her face. 'No Inspector. I can't recall the name.'

He nodded. 'That's all right. I just wondered. Well, I must be off. Thanks for the tea.'

Ten minutes later he was in his office at Bromersley police station.

He picked up the phone and dialled a number. 'Cadet Ahaz? . . . Will you find him and send him to my office, straight away?'

Angel looked down at the correspondence on his desk. There was a tap at the door.

'Come in.'

It was Ahmed. He came in breathing heavily. 'I saw you arrive, sir. I came straight away. I thought you might want me for something.'

'I do. Where have you been? You're harder to find than Shergar.'

Ahmed's eyes opened wide. His eyebrows shot up. 'What's Shergar, sir?'

'Never mind, lad. Never mind,' he replied impatiently and buried his head in the papers on his desk. Without looking up he said, 'That Citroen car belonging to Lady Millhouse has been stolen. You have the number?'

'Yes, sir.'

'Have it put on the stolen car list. Do you know how to do that?'

'Yes, sir.' Ahmed turned to go.

'Report that it will be found locally, somewhere near Bradford Road, I expect,' he murmured, deeply engrossed in a letter.

'Bradford Road in Bromersley, sir?'

'Yes, lad. That's where they'll find it,' he said patiently. 'Here in this town.'

Ahmed opened the door and then slowly turned back to the inspector. 'How do you know that, sir?'

ELEVEN

'Come in, Ron.' Angel said. 'Sit down.'

'Thank you, sir,' Gawber said, pulling up a chair.

'What did Mac say?' He asked eagerly.

'He said it looks like Scrap Scudamore was hit on the head and then asphyxiated. He has severe bruising on the throat consistent with a man's fingers enclosing his windpipe and both thumbs pressing on his trachea. He thought there was some damage to the skull, but you know him, he wanted to wait for an X-ray before committing himself.'

'A blow to the head before asphyxiation would possibly have rendered Scudamore dazed or unconscious, allowing a less powerful man easily to choke him to death. He's a big lump is Scudamore. I wouldn't have liked to take him on single handedly.'

DS Gawber nodded.

'And Mac says it would be a man?'

'He seems certain of it. The severity of the bruises, and the space between the bruises.'

Angel nodded. The corners of his mouth turned down. He leaned back in his chair. He put his arms behind his head and arched his back. After a moment he said thoughtfully, 'A choker?'

'Yes, sir.'

'The same man who murdered Yvette Millhouse,' he said quietly.

'Looks like it, sir.'

'The choker.'

Gawber nodded.

'Did Mac give any indication of the time of death?'

'No, sir.'

'Did he think the body had been moved?'

'He didn't say, but I got the impression that he thought it had happened there.'

Angel rubbed his chin. 'Mmm. I'll phone him later. Did you get anything out of the house to house?'

'No, sir. Nothing.'

'Anything more from the man with the dog who found the body?'

'No, sir.'

'What about Scudamore's movements? Did anybody know anything?'

'I spoke to several people including the landlord of The Feathers. He had been in there, drinking with his brother, Scott and several others. He'd also been seen in conversation with Duncan Millhouse until about nine o'clock when they left and went up to the Can Can Club together. Nobody seems to have noticed what time Scudamore left but he was still there at eleven-thirty.'

Suddenly Angel leaned forward and put his hands on the desk. He wrinkled his nose and said, 'I do hate this job.' Then he asked quickly, 'Where's Scrap Scudamore's car? It's an old Jaguar, didn't you tell me?'

'Yes, sir. He keeps it in the street, outside his house. Mac's probably going over it right now.'

The phone rang. The inspector reached over the desk.

'Angel,' he snapped.

It was the PC on the reception desk.

'Yes? What is it, lad? . . . Who? . . . Scott Scudamore?'

Angel and Gawber exchanged glances.

'What's he want, lad? . . . Well, tell him I'm out, but Detective Sergeant Gawber who is working on the case can spare him a minute. He knows him . . . Right, lad. He's coming out now.'

Gawber stood up and put the chair back by the wall.

Angel replaced the phone. His eyes shone with surprise. 'Scott Scudamore! Who would have thought it? Anyway, you can deal with him. It's an opportunity to ask him about last night.' The inspector looked at Gawber sternly. 'And Ron, make a point of reminding him that we have got Harry Hull for that off-licence robbery and that it's only that very fragile alibi provided by his girlfriend, what's her name—'

'Annabelle,' Gawber said.

'Aye, Annabelle or Bella, as she likes to be known — that's keeping him from slopping out in Strangeways.'

'Right, sir,' Gawber said with his hand on the door.

'Lay it on thick. Let him know in no uncertain terms that it's only a matter of time before he'll be behind bars. You can't over state, Ron. Something's got to make him crack. I want him behind bars.'

'Yes, sir.'

'If it isn't pressure from Annabelle, then it'll be pressure from me!' he bellowed.

There was no reply.

'And tell him Mrs Patel is still on antidepressants!' he yelled.

The door was closed. DS Gawber had gone. Angel shook his head and muttered. 'You need more patience than a zoo-keeper waiting for Pandas to mate.'

The phone rang.

'Now what?' he growled into the mouthpiece.

It was an internal call. It was the duty PC in charge of the cells. Simone Lyon wanted to see DI Angel. Apparently she had been pestering the PC all morning. He had ignored her request but now she was screaming.

Angel's eyebrows lifted. He had been waiting for Simone Lyon to ask to see him. He recalled the old saying, 'All things come to those who wait.' He hoped the wait had been worth his while. 'Right, Constable. Show her into an interview room. I'll come down straight away.'

Angel picked up the audiotape from the table behind his chair and made his way down the corridor.

Simone Lyon duly arrived. Her hair not as meticulously groomed as before. Her face was flushed and her lips set as if she had kissed a lemon.

She glared at Angel who glared back at her. He silently indicated a chair and switched on the recording machine.

They sat in silence for a few seconds and then Angel said, 'Well?'

She said nothing.

At that moment, he wanted a cigarette more than any-thing else in the world. He had to content himself with merely moistening his lips. 'The constable said you wanted to see me?'

She looked down and then up. She put her elbows on the table. Her slim, manicured hands were shaking. Suddenly she dropped her hands to her lap and began to speak very quickly.

'I want to know how much longer you intend keeping me in that dreadful cell?'

'Well at least until your case comes before a court. That might be a month or two yet,' he lied, looking her straight in the eye.

She blew out a short gasp. 'No!' She shook her head several times. Her long black hair marked with wisps of grey swirled from side to side. There was a moment or two of silence then she looked up and said, 'What must I do?'

'Simply tell me why you attempted to poison Sir Charles Millhouse.'

She shook her head. 'I would convict myself if I did that, Inspector.'

'No you wouldn't. Your situation could not be any worse than it is now. Two policemen saw you put poison in Sir Charles Millhouse's glass. He would have drunk from it if I had not knocked it out of his hand. That evidence on its own will convict you. And the evidence is quite undeniable!'

He waited.

She nodded thoughtfully.

He went on. 'There might be some extenuating circumstance that would allow me to drop the charge or enable your counsel to offer mitigating evidence to limit or reduce any sentence you may be awarded by a judge. But the fact is irrefutable.' He hesitated before speaking further. 'You know, you really need a solicitor.'

'That's all right. I trust you. You have an honest face.'

He looked at the rotating spool of tape and allowed himself a small smile, as he thought how that last comment would look on the witness's statement.

She went on. 'As you say, I was caught in the act, so there is no point in pretending that I didn't put the poison in the glass. There is also no point in suggesting that I didn't know that the glass belonged to Sir Charles Millhouse. I had seen his photograph often enough. He was never out of the papers. God knows!'

Her hands shook. She began pulling the handkerchief tightly between her hands, then releasing it. Then repeating the operation.

Angel looked at her gently.

She went on. 'But you have to understand that not only has my daughter been murdered by that man, but that her father was also murdered by him.'

She stopped and swallowed.

Angel noticed his heartbeat was beginning to thump. 'Tell me about it,' he said quietly.

'I will try to tell it in chronological order. I was born in Paris. My father was a baker by trade. My mother helped him in the shop. We were lower class struggling to be middle class. My parents had great ambitions for me. They sent me to a good school. I had extra lessons in foreign languages, notably English, deportment, ballet and so on. I secured employment initially as a secretary in magazine publishing. I met a lot of men and had several lovers. One of them was very special. He was a lot older than I was. His name was Marcus La Touche. He became the father of my only child, my daughter, Yvette. He was in the banking business. He had liaisons with merchant banks over here, and he spent a lot of time in London. This was twenty-five years ago. In the course of his activities he met Charles Millhouse, as he was then. He had a flat in London. They became good friends. Marcus used to stay with Charles Millhouse in Yorkshire occasionally. They used to have wild parties. Marcus used to say that champagne flowed like water. One night, while they were on a spree in London, Charles drove his powerful sports car into a wall. Marcus was seriously injured. He had a fractured skull. Charles was only slightly hurt and left hospital with a few bandages. Marcus lived for two days. I flew across from Paris. He lived long enough to tell me all about the crash. Charles didn't admit it was his fault. He didn't visit Marcus in hospital even though they had been such good friends. All he suffered was a driving ban for life. He's had to employ a chauffeur ever since. Huh! Our daughter, Yvette was fifteen years old. She adored her father, as I did. Our world collapsed. I was not his wife so I had no claim on his estate. We had a struggling time in Paris. I was trying to find suitable work and bring up my daughter on my own. The years rolled by, as they do. Yvette grew up and vowed she would avenge her father's death. She came over to England, sought Charles out, discovered he was a widower, forged a relationship with him and in August last they were married.'

She hesitated and lowered her eyes.

Angel said, 'And then she tried to murder him by poisoning him with rat poison!'

She looked up. Her eyes opened wide. 'You know?'

'It wasn't difficult to work out. Please go on.'

'Well, Charles must have found out. Yvette did tell me that he had been ill and had been to the hospital, and that she would have to be careful. That was three weeks ago. And that was her last letter to me. I never heard from her again. I became very worried. The next thing I saw splashed across the French newspapers was that the body of Lady Yvette Millhouse had been found in a reservoir.'

Her hands shook. She momentarily pulled the handkerchief between them and then relaxed the grip. She dabbed her nose and said, 'Obviously, Charles Millhouse had discovered Yvette's identity and her attempt to er—'

She stopped again and breathed out a long sigh.

Angel shook his head. 'To murder him. So you came over determined to finish the job?'

She straightened up. 'No!' she replied emphatically. 'Certainly not. No. I merely wanted to continue administering the small doses so that no one would suspect Yvette of attempting to murder him. After all, if his illness flared up again, and after her death then obviously Yvette could not have been responsible. It would remove her from the field of suspicion. That is all I wanted to do. I swear it. You will see that I booked my return flight to Paris for today, because obviously I had intended to return home today. The ticket is in my handbag. You can see for yourself. If I had been intending murdering Charles I would have stayed until he was dead, wouldn't I?' Angel did not reply.

She continued. 'On top of everything else, Inspector, if it came out that Yvette had been thought to be a murderer, that would have been very hard for me to bear.'

Angel said quietly, 'Well, I'm afraid you'll have to face up to that now.'

'I know. But I didn't expect to be caught in the act.'

She sat back in her chair and dabbed her nose with her handkerchief. Her breathing was even. She was relaxed now, relieved at having told her story.

'Have you anything else to tell me?'

'No, I don't think so, Inspector,' she replied wiping an eye with the back of her hand. 'Do I get released now?'

He looked down at her and smiled. 'I will have to consult the chief constable. It may be possible to let you out on bail pending any charges. You would have to surrender your passport and be available for further questioning, if it should be necessary.'

She nodded. 'How long for?'

'Say, a week,' he replied with an avuncular smile. 'What is the accommodation at The Feathers like?'

'Could I stay there?'

'I think so.'

She allowed herself a small smile. 'It's better than here!'

Angel stood up. He summoned the duty jailer. Simone Lyon was led back to her cell.

Angel returned to his office. His mind was racing. The facts he had been juggling with that past week were falling into place. There was a lot to do.

At last he had a motive.

* * *

Detective Sergeant Ron Gawber grinned. 'That's great news, sir.'

Angel nodded and leaned forward out of the chair. 'I shall want to see Sir Charles at a very early date, but I don't want his suspicions raised. I don't intend issuing a warrant at this stage. I want you to find out from his housekeeper when he is due back from London. Don't let it sound urgent. I'll arrange to see him then. We still have to play this very carefully, Ron. We have the motive but we haven't got a watertight case,' he said stabbing the desktop with his forefinger. 'There is still the chance he could wriggle free. We need to establish that his wife was murdered by him — in the Hall or elsewhere — was undressed and rolled in the carpet by him and then transported to Western Beck by him. Well, we can prove that he murdered her, but I'm not sure that we can prove that he took her body up to Western Beck yet. For one thing he doesn't drive!'

'He probably can, but he doesn't.'

'Right. I'll go along with that.'

'He hasn't been seen driving a car.'

'Precisely. But what vehicle would he have used to transport the body? I believe that her body was rolled in the carpet, and that the carpet and the body were taken up to Western Beck.'

'That's right, sir. But Mac said that there were no carpet fibres in any of the family cars, the Rolls, the Citroen, or the Mercedes.'

'So that means that either she was not rolled in the carpet to take her body up to the reservoir, or that the vehicle used to transport the body is as yet unknown to us.'

'Mmm. Or Mac is wrong, and he has simply overlooked any traces of fibre, or simply, that there weren't any.'

'Have you ever known Mac to be wrong?'

Gawber shook his head.

Angel continued quickly. 'Nor have I. And I have known him more than twenty years. And that old piece of carpet would have shed some tell-tale fibres wherever it had been carried. I'm certain of that! Very well. Then we are left with the possibility that Yvette Millhouse had been carried naked out of the house to a car or a vehicle of some sort and then in turn taken out of the vehicle naked at Western Beck and dumped into the water. That would have been unnecessarily risky, and pointless. A roll of carpet is ideal cover for moving a body about. And what would be the point of taking a piece of carpet up to Western Beck if it didn't have a useful purpose? No. It doesn't make sense.'

Gawber nodded.

'Then I take it that you agree with me, that Yvette Millhouse *was* definitely transported rolled in the carpet.'

'Yes, sir.'

'Then we have to find the vehicle that took it there.'

They both nodded.

Gawber said, 'Where do we start?'

Angel stroked his chin.

There was a knock at the door.

'Come in,' Angel called.

It was Cadet Ahmed Ahaz. He put his head through the door. He smiled across at Angel and Gawber. He was holding a piece of paper. 'Excuse me, sir. Excuse me, Sergeant.' He came into the room up to Angel and held out the paper. 'You were right, sir. But I don't know how you did it.'

'What is it, lad?' He said taking the paper.

'A Panda car has found that missing Citroen, sir. You said it would be found near Bradford Road, and it was. How did you do that, sir?' Ahmed asked excitedly.

Angel smiled at Ahmed as he took the report from him. 'Guesswork, lad. Guesswork.'

Ahmed blinked.

'Come in, lad. Close that door and wait over there.' He pointed to the chair by the cupboard.

Angel read the report and turned to Gawber with raised eyebrows. 'That didn't take long. No damage was done to it. It was found locked. The seat was set back for a big person. Well it would have been set forward for Lady Yvette, wouldn't it? She was only short. No fingerprints. I would have been surprised if there had been.' He lowered the report and looked up. 'Ahmed.'

'Yes, sir.'

'Tell the duty transport officer that when Scenes of Crime have finished with that Citroen that I want it moving off the street, today, before it is dark, and taken up to Millhouse Hall. All right.'

'Yes, sir,' he replied smiling. He stood there looking at the inspector still smiling.

'Go on then. Pronto!'

'Oh yes sir. Pronto!' Ahmed said. He dashed through the door and closed it quietly.

Angel looked at Gawber and then shook his head.

Gawber smiled and then said, 'I've been thinking, sir. It's getting to look as if Sir Charles took the car. He could have left for London in the Rolls chauffeured by Melanie Bright, come back by train, and taken the Citroen to the Can Can Club to await Scrap Scudamore.'

'Mmm. What would he use for a key? Shouldn't think he could hot wire a car.'

'Every car has two keys, sir. No doubt there would be a spare key at the Hall?'

Angel's eyebrows shot up. 'And all the time we would think he was in London?'

'Exactly.'

'A good alibi, the foundation stone of a crime.'

Gawber nodded.

Angel pursed his lips. 'How would he get back to the railway station from the back of the Can Can Club?'

'By taxi, sir?'

'Well, check up on that. There are only about twenty taxis in Bromersley. There would only be about half a dozen working through the night. That shouldn't be difficult.'

'Right, sir. I'll get on to it.' Gawber stood up to go. He could smell a breakthrough.

Angel said, 'Just a minute, what did Scott Scudamore want?'

Gawber brightened. 'He wanted to complain that the police were not protecting the innocent tax paying citizens of this town, and that it was not safe for a man to walk the street without risk of being murdered. He also wanted to know if we would be looking through Scrap's things, and when—'

Angel jumped in quickly. 'Put a guard on that house today and tonight.'

'I've done that, sir.'

'Good. Go on.'

'And when could he have access to the house, he said, as he was next of kin!'

'He's not without cheek. Anything else?'

'No, sir.'

'Did you tell him what I told you to tell him?'

'Yes sir.'

'Andy?'

Gawber hesitated and then smiled. 'I can't repeat exactly what he said, sir, but the second word was, "off".'

Angel stared at him and grunted. 'Huh. I've got a degree in rudeness. Learned at the Inland Revenue College of Charm and Charisma. I'll take him on anytime he likes.'

The sergeant grinned. He didn't reply.

Angel added, 'In fact the sooner, the better. I don't understand it. He ought to be nice to us. It would be in his best interests to be friendly to the police, instead of making enemies of us. Perhaps we would be nicer to him. I don't know.' Angel muttered something incomprehensible and then said loudly, 'You know, Scott Scudamore's got more slates missing than Strangeways.'

Gawber nodded.

'And it was Tinker Scudamore — his father — who was on the roof in 1976 chucking them down!'

Gawber smiled as he stood up. 'I'd better get on, sir. And I'll check on those taxis tonight.'

'Right,' Angel said curtly. He reached across the desk and picked up a pile of papers. 'On your way past the CID room, call in and tell that cadet I want him?'

'Yes, sir.'

The door closed.

Angel threw down the papers and reached into his pocket and pulled out a small packet. It had a green and white labelled wrapper covering a sealed silver paper sachet. The printing on the sleeve read 'Nicotine chewing gum. Contains no sugar.' He pulled off the sleeve and then attempted to tear open the silver paper. The packet resisted. He tried digging in his fingernails and pulling. He tried several times. He made no impression. It could not be opened. Eventually he managed to make a small tear in the silver paper. He kept pulling at it. It resisted. He tried several times. Then, unexpectedly, the paper tore open and the contents of white torpedo shaped tablets spewed out across the desk. He quickly put one in his mouth and sunk his teeth into it.

There was a knock at the door.

Angel quickly gathered up the loose sticks of gum and swept them into a drawer.

'Come in.'

It was Cadet Ahmed Ahaz.

'You wanted me, sir?'

'Yes. Bring me the London street map from the CID office.'

'Are you going away, sir?'

'No, I'm not. You ask more questions than my wife!' he said with a wave of the hand. 'Hurry up!'

'Yes, sir. Pronto,' he said. He went out and closed the door.

Angel quickly opened his desk drawer and picked out the loose nicotine chewing gum tablets and put them into an envelope and stuffed them quickly into his pocket.

There was a knock on the door.

He reached out for the pile of correspondence and then called out, 'Come in.'

It was Cadet Ahmed Ahaz again. He was carrying the A-to-Z street guide of London. 'Was that pronto enough for you, sir?' He said with a smile, and he held up the front of the book for Angel to see. 'Is this what you wanted, sir?'

Angel looked up from the letters. 'Yes, that's it, lad. Ta. Put it there,' he said pointing to the desk.

Ahmed went out of the room and closed the door.

Angel tossed the pile of correspondence on one side and reached over for the street guide urgently. 'Now then, Marylebone Road. What page is it?'

He fingered through the pages, found the reference and then the map. His finger traced across the map. A few seconds later, he found what he was looking for. He leaned back in the chair and beamed. Then he closed the street guide and placed it on the corner of his desk nearest the door. He leaned back in the chair and looked at the ceiling. He closed his eyes briefly and wondered what Charles Millhouse might have been doing around Marylebone Road.

The phone rang.

He sighed, leaned forward and picked up the receiver. 'Angel.'

It was the WPC on the telephone switchboard. 'Inspector, there's an odd person on the line. Her name is Annie Potts. She asked if you were in. I didn't say that you were. She wants to speak to you.'

'That's all right, Constable. Put her through.'

There was a click. 'Hello. Angel here. Is that you Annie?'

'Oh yes. I'm glad you are in.'

She sounded breathless. 'Can I speak to you a minute, Mr Angel?'

'Of course you can. Is there something wrong? Where are you speaking from?'

'I'm at home Mr Angel. Oh dear! I've just come back from the shop. A woman in there said that that man, Scrap Scudamore had been found murdered at the side of the Can Can Club. Is that right? I know *you'd* know.'

'Yes, it's right, Annie. Why?'

'Well, it must have happened last night.'

'Yes, Annie. It did.'

'Well, you remember I told you about overhearing him talking to that Duncan Millhouse, last Wednesday night, and I was telling you what he said about you, among other things?'

'Yes.'

'Well, I was in the The Feathers with my friend, Edie Longstaff again, last night. And would you believe it, they came in *again* and sat right next to us *again.'* She paused and pushed the handset closer to her ear. Then she said quickly, 'are you there?'

'Yes, Annie. I'm listening.'

'Yes. Well, that Scrap Scudamore and Duncan Millhouse were drinking as if whisky was going out of fashion. Especially that Scudamore! And who do you think was doing all the buying? Duncan Millhouse was doing all the buying, I tell you. I don't think that Scudamore put 'is 'and to 'is pocket all evening.' She took another deep breath and then waited. 'Are you there?'

'I hear you, Annie.'

'Ah, yes. Right. Well, I *had* to tell you. They were talking about money. I couldn't make it out exactly. A lot of money. Ten thousand pounds was mentioned! I ask you, Mr Angel, who's got ten thousand pounds in Bromersley now that the mines are closed down? Anyway, that Scudamore kept going on about it. I don't know if they was planning to rob a bank together or what. They were very chummy. Very chummy indeed. That Scudamore also said something about it would be worse if she was expecting. Well *he* said pregnant. I couldn't catch who he was talking about. I couldn't work out whether it was Duncan Millhouse's wife that was expecting, or somebody else. Or nobody. I'm not too sure about that part of it. Can you hear me, Mr Angel?'

'I hear you, Annie. I hear you.'

'He *definitely* said ten thousand pounds, Mr Angel. But who would be pregnant?'

TWELVE

Angel turned his car into Sebastopol Terrace: a long stretch of high-roofed houses with many small black windows overlooking a side street sadly in need of repair. Old cars of mixed sizes were parked on both sides of the road. A police car, and a black van from Scenes of Crime added to the congestion. A young, uniformed policeman was standing at the open doorway of the end house.

Two women in floral aprons with scarves wound tightly around their heads stood on their respective front steps with their arms folded, chattering to each other. When they saw Angel's shiny car approach, they stopped talking and blatantly stared across at him. Two small girls bounced brightly coloured rubber balls on the pavement and then on the house walls cyclically.

Angel found a space at the far end of the street, between two old cars. He locked his car and walked back up the street to the policeman.

He threw him up a salute. 'Good morning, sir.'

'Morning, lad. This has got to be the place where Scrap Scudamore had a flat?'

'Yes, sir.'

'Is Dr Mac there?'

'Yes.' He turned round and looked through the open door. 'I think he's coming out just now, sir.'

The compact figure of Dr Mac emerged through the green painted street door. He was in white overalls, close-fitting hat and white boots. He was carrying a green plastic bag. His spectacles were his most distinguishing feature. He hovered on the front step when he saw the inspector.

'It's you, Mick.'

'How's it going? Find anything interesting?'

'Not yet. What were you expecting?'

'I dunno. Swag would be useful. Although we can hardly charge him now, can we?' He grinned.

'Haven't found anything like that, Mick. Just the usual domestic bits and pieces of a man living on his own.'

'No signs of a woman then?'

Mac smiled. 'A few dirty photographs, that's all.'

Angel looked disappointed.

'We'll be through here by this afternoon. I'll let you know if I find the Grand Cham's diamond.'

'Ta. What about the postmortem on him? Have you finished that?'

'It's being typed up.'

'Can you give me the gist?'

'Aye. He died from asphyxia. He was choked to death.'

'The murderer would have had to be male then, I suppose?'

'I think it was male from the placing of the bruises, but, in this case, you canna be certain.'

'How's that?'

Dr Mac smiled. 'Do you happen to know if he was celebrating something big that night?'

Angel screwed up his eyebrows. 'No.' Then he added, 'The only big thing he would have to celebrate would be the size of his head!'

'His bloodstream had the highest alcohol content of all my customers I can recall for some time. You can understand why vampires enjoy their work.' He smiled and then added, 'It must have been a woman then. I hope she'd been worth it.'

'Oh, I think she had.' Angel said. He was thinking of Melanie Bright.

'Well, the victim received a fractured skull at the back, consistent with having a corner faced object, such as a house brick, being either dropped, thrown or held in the hand and wielded with a mighty force. It would have stunned the brain, causing temporary (or permanent) paralysis of the muscles with loss of balance, resulting in him falling. In such a feeble state, a much weaker person could easily have applied their hands to his throat and choked him to death.'

Angel nodded thoughtfully. He didn't speak for a few seconds. 'So he was choked to death?'

'Aye.'

'Similar to Lady Yvette Millhouse?'

'Nae. Not similar, Michael,' the white-haired Scot said heavily. 'I'd bet my feyther's second best set of pipes that it was the same man.'

Dr Mac turned away and made his way to the black van.

Angel followed. His hands thrust into his pockets. His eyes looked down at the cracks in the flagstones.

The doctor slid open the side door of the van and deposited the big green plastic bag he had brought out of the house.

Angel looked up at the small man in the white clothes and said, 'Scudamore had a car?'

Mac turned round and pointed to a big, black Jaguar saloon, a few cars away. 'Aye. That one. If you can call it a car.'

Angel turned to look at it.

'Have you been over it?'

Mac nodded. 'Help yourself.'

'Thanks, Mac. I will have a look. Hear from you when you're ready.'

He waved at the doctor without looking.

'Aye.'

Then the inspector walked systematically round the powerful old car. The number plate indicated that the black saloon was more than twenty years old. There were signs of an old accident, an indentation and a wide scratch on the nearside door, and one of the tyres was flat. There were old newspapers screwed up on the floor in the back. Angel thought they were fish and chip papers. The leather upholstery was cracked in several places. There was a worn cushion on the front seat. He stopped and peered at the tax disc. It was still licenced. His eyebrows lifted. He tried the door. It was locked. He went round to the rear. He tried the tailgate door. It opened. He raised it to its full height. The smell of rancid fish and chips billowed round his nostrils. The boot was empty. He pulled a face and grunted as he lifted the thick carpet and the false bottom between his finger and thumb. He was looking for the spare wheel. He found the studs sticking up that would have held it. There was a jack, a handle and a spanner, but no spare wheel. He let go of the false bottom and then looked across the grubby carpet to assess the size of the boot. He nodded almost imperceptibly. He lowered the tailgate door. It made a solid clunk as it closed.

Angel looked down at the flat tyre again. His jaw tightened. He licked his lips and patted his pockets hoping some kind angel had dropped a packet of cigarettes in one of them.

They hadn't.

* * *

Sir Charles Millhouse bounced into the drawing room carrying a glass of an amber liquid. He looked very smart in a light brown tweed suit, red dickie bow and white shirt. He was wiping perspiration from his forehead with a crisply ironed white handkerchief. The gold signet ring on his little finger caught the light from the table lamp by Angel's chair and twinkled briefly as he raised his glass.

'Yes Inspector. Mrs Moore said you wanted to see me.'

Angel looked up from a comfortable armchair facing the grandfather clock. He switched on his best disarming smile as he made to stand up. 'Good evening, sir.'

'Please, don't get up. Good evening. Look here, Inspector, I have only just arrived home. What brings you here? It's been one hell of a week in the House. I hope it is important.'

'Oh yes, Sir Charles. I have a few questions, nothing more,' he replied airily, with the wave of the hand. 'My sergeant phoned earlier in the week to find out when you would be back in Bromersley. Your housekeeper said you would be back from London this afternoon. So here I am. I could have summoned you back from London, you know, but I try to be considerate,' he said pointedly.

Sir Charles's manner softened. 'Well, yes. I appreciate that, Inspector.' He took a sip from the glass. 'Oh. Can I offer you a drink? A whisky or . . . ?'

'No thanks.'

178

Sir Charles chose a comfortable chair almost opposite the policeman. 'Are you any nearer finding my wife's murderer?'

Angel nodded. 'Indeed we are, I'm pleased to say. Indeed we are. There are just a few little details.'

'Yes. Yes. Good. Well, fire away, Inspector.'

The grandfather clock chimed the quarter. Angel's head swivelled round to look at the dial. His eyes travelled down the dark polished oak case all the way to the floor.

'A beautiful clock,' he said looking down at its foot. 'Yes. Yes.' Sir Charles said quickly, looking at his watch. And it's spot on time.'

Angel's eyes appeared to see something interesting.

'Excuse me,' he said, as he raised himself out of the chair. He kneeled down on the plush carpet and leaned forward towards the bottom of the clock. 'I thought I saw something shining at me.'

'What is the matter,' Sir Charles said looking intently.

Angel looked back to check that he was being observed by the man.

He was.

Then he put his finger through the cutaway part of the clock case and slowly manoeuvred into the light the tiny pearl he had deliberately placed there six days earlier.

'Whatever is it?'

'It's a pearl!' Angel said as he rose to his feet. 'I wonder how that got there?'

Sir Charles stood up. 'A pearl?' His mouth opened and stayed open.

Angel held it between finger and thumb. He offered it to Sir Charles, who held out his hand. Angel released it into his palm.

Sir Charles held it as if it had been a ten-carat diamond instead of a tiny glass bead dipped in lacquer. But he wasn't to know. He sat down. His eyes lowered.

'You know what this is, inspector, don't you?'

'No, Sir Charles,' he lied. 'Tell me.'

'A pearl from my wife's choker. The one she always wore.' Sir Charles gazed at it fondly.

'Oh?' Angel said. He knew he must move cautiously. He silently counted to ten and then he said, innocently, 'I wonder how it got there.'

Sir Charles held the pearl up for the light to reflect from it. After a few seconds, he shook his head slowly as he closed his fist tightly round the imitation pearl. He looked down at the carpet, recently cleaned and returned to the front of the fireplace, and then to the foot of the clock. He stood up. His eyes moved slowly from side to side. He walked to the drawing room door tapping the side of his thumb on his lips. He turned round. He came back and looked across at Angel. His mouth opened as if he was about to speak. He changed his mind and turned away. He walked to the door again, and then suddenly he turned round and thrust his arms into the air.

'Oh no!!' he yelled. Then he held his head in his hands for a second and slumped in a chair.

Angel knew what was going through Sir Charles Millhouse's mind.

They sat together in silence.

After a minute, Sir Charles said quietly, 'You know who murdered Yvette, don't you, Inspector?'

Angel nodded. 'I do now, sir.'

* * *

It was the following morning.

Sir Charles Millhouse had made a statement and was in a cell at the station. Inspector Angel's team at Bromersley police station

180

was glowing with success. Detective Inspector Angel almost ran into his office. The door was open and he was humming a Frank Sinatra song of yesteryear called, 'I Did It My Way.'

Cadet Ahmed Ahaz put his nose through the open door. 'I've got your post, sir,' he said, opening the door wider.

'Thank you, Ahmed,' he beamed and carried on humming.

Ahmed placed the letters on the desk. 'Things are going well for you, sir?'

'Couldn't be better, lad,' he said looking up. Ahmed came closer to the big man. His smile was bigger than ever. 'Would it be a good time then to ask you about my promotion, sir? Will you be putting a letter of recommendation about me to the chief constable? My mother says I should not let the grass grow under my feet, sir. That I should strike while the iron is hot. And that there is no time like the present.'

Angel chuckled. He tried to conceal his amusement from the cadet. He looked down at the correspondence. 'Your mother is quite right. I'll look into it. In the meantime, I want you to buzz off and keep busy. Can you do that?'

'Keep busy, sir?' he said, raising his eyebrows.

'As busy as a flea in a nightdress.'

'Oh yes, sir,' he beamed, dashed out of the office and closed the door.

The inspector reached out for the letters. The phone rang. He reached out for the receiver. 'Angel.'

It was Ron Gawber. 'Good morning, sir.'

'Morning, Ron. Where are you?'

'Scrap Scudamore's flat, sir. We've just made a discovery. Under a loose floorboard under the bed is a black plastic bin liner. Inside is the damaged pearl choker, loose pearls from it, a red woollen jumper, ladies jeans, shoes, underwear and a handbag.'

Angel's eyebrows went up. 'Great! Get them to Mac as soon as possible.'

'Will do. I couldn't wait to tell you.'

'You did right, Ron.'

He could hear the sound of triumphalism in his voice. 'It wraps up the case against Scrap Scudamore beautifully, doesn't it?'

'Magnificently, Ron. Magnificently. Tell me, is there a car key in the handbag?'

'No sir. It has the usual stuff, but no money and no keys.'

'I didn't think there would be.'

'There's something else, sir.'

'Yes?'

'You remember we needed to know how Sir Charles would get from the Can Can Club to the railway station? And we thought it would have to be by taxi?'

'Yes.'

'Well, last night I went round all the taxi offices and asked all the drivers working that night and no one could remember him. Now then, sir, they would have remembered Sir Charles Millhouse, wouldn't they? I mean, he's not your usual nighttime drunk, is he?'

'Well it doesn't matter now, Ron, does it?'

'Just thought I'd tell you, sir.'

'Right, lad.'

'Bye.'

He replaced the receiver and rubbed his hands like a moneylender in a miner's strike.

The phone rang again. He reached out for it eagerly. 'Angel.'

It was Doctor Mac. 'Yes, laddie. I've got some news for you.'

'You're on the wagon?' He said teasingly.

182

'Tosh. No!' he replied. 'And if you're in a daft mood, I'm nae talking to you.'

'Go on, Mac. You sound sober.'

'I've found fibres from that piece of carpet we pulled out of Western Beck in the boot of Scrap Scudamore's car — that old Jaguar.'

'That's great, Mac. That confirms that Lady Yvette's body was taken from the Hall to Western Beck in that old car, just as I thought. You're a genius.'

'Maybe I am. Jus' doing my job,' he replied in that sing-song Scottish accent peculiar to Glasgow. 'And there's something else, laddie. I think you'd like to know.'

'Yes, Mac. What's that?'

'I found a car key in Scrap Scudamore's jacket pocket. And it was nae for a Jaguar car. No. It was for a Citroen. And it was nae for any old Citroen. I sent a man up to the Hall with it, and it fits the Millhouse's Citroen!'

Angel beamed. 'That's great, Mac. Thanks very much. That confirms that he took the Citroen. That's what I thought when I saw the flat tyre and no spare. I'll tell Flora MacDonald when I see her.'

Angel returned the phone to its cradle. He leaned back in the chair. Unusually, he found himself smiling. Everything was going to plan. Things couldn't be better. The only thing missing was a cigarette. He leaned forward to the drawer and helped himself to a strip of nicotine chewing gum. It would hold the craving at bay for a while. He folded it and put it in his mouth. He sunk his teeth into the yellow stuff and sighed. There is no denying that it was going to be very satisfying to put this case to the Crown Prosecution Service.

The phone rang. He leaned forward and picked up the handset. 'Angel.'

It was the WPC at the reception desk. 'Inspector, there's a man here asking to see Sir Charles Millhouse. He says he's his son, Duncan Millhouse. Is it all right?' She sounded unusually crisp. Maybe Duncan had been rubbing her up the wrong way.

'Thank you, Constable. I'll send someone to collect him.'

'Right, sir.'

There was a click. Angel had a clear line. He dialled out a number.

Ahmed answered. 'Cadet Ahaz, I would be pleased to assist you.'

Angel couldn't resist a smile. He was not used to such courtesy in the police station. 'Ahmed, there's a man at reception, a Mr Duncan Millhouse, will you show him down to my office straight away?'

'I will, sir,' he said brightly. Then he added the word, 'Pronto!'

Angel returned the receiver to its cradle and then stood up. He gathered together the papers on his desk and rammed them in a drawer. He dropped an empty paper cup into the wastepaper basket and then looked round the room. Everything was tidy. He looked in the mirror and noticed an unruly twist of hair sticking out like a flag from the side of his head. He tried to flatten it with his hand. It refused to stay down. There was a knock. He turned to face the door.

'Come in,' he said quickly and forgot the hair.

It was Cadet Ahaz. His eyes were unusually wide open and shining, and his jaw was set. 'Mr Millhouse, sir,' he hissed through clenched teeth.

Angel noticed Ahmed's unusual manner. He said nothing, and with a nod of the head indicated to him that he should leave them alone.

The cadet closed the door.

THIRTEEN

Duncan Millhouse was dressed in an expensive suit and shirt but still managed to look untidy. He suffered from four o'clock shadow and was in need of a shave.

When the two men were on their own, the inspector held out his hand to the young man. 'Good morning, Mr Millhouse.'

Duncan Millhouse looked back at the door and then at Angel. 'Good morning,' he said automatically. 'I want to see my father.'

'Yes, I know,' Angel said with that deceitful smile he had practised so well. 'I'd just like to ask you a few questions. Just to tidy up a few loose ends. Is that all right?'

'I suppose so,' he replied looking at his wristwatch. 'Will it take long?'

'No. Let's go into the interview room.'

Angel picked up a tape from his desktop and passed swiftly across the front of the man to the door. 'After you, sir.'

Duncan looked annoyed. He didn't reply. He went along with the inspector's request.

When they were seated in the interview room and formalities over, Angel said, 'There was a slight misunderstanding that occurred in the interview you gave me in my office a couple of days ago. I expect it's only an oversight. I am sure you can put me right in a jiffy.'

Duncan Millhouse looked surprised. He looked anxiously around the room. 'Oh? What's that then?'

Angel looked him square in the face and, with a smile, said, 'I asked you if you went out at all on the evening of your stepmother's funeral.'

Millhouse screwed up his face as if he was trying to remember.

Angel dipped into his inside pocket and brought out his leather-backed notebook, already open at the appropriate page. 'You said,' he began reading, 'I quote: "Well, I wasn't outside the back of the Can Can Club, I can tell you that. I was at home with Susan, my wife. We were there all evening and all night. We didn't go out. I had just been to my stepmother's funeral. I was not in the best sorts." '

Angel lowered the book and smiled across at him.

He glowered back.

'Well, Mr Millhouse? Is that correct?'

'Of course!'

Angel pursed his lips. 'I have a statement from two witnesses who say you were in The Feathers that night.'

Duncan immediately began to perspire. He passed his hand through his thick hair. 'Oh? I must have just dropped in for a drink.'

'And that you were with Scrap Scudamore!'

He held up his hands as if to protect an assault on his face. 'No. No. That's not true. Those two old biddies got it wrong.'

'Which two old biddies?'

'I wasn't with Scrap Scudamore.'

Angel's face changed. He dropped the smile and pseudo charm. He looked straight into the younger man's steel blue eyes. 'I'll let you into a little secret, shall I?'

Duncan's jaw dropped.

'Your father isn't in here because he murdered two people. Oh no. He's here as my guest. For the one night only. For his own protection. He's being protected from you!'

Duncan's lip quivered. 'You can't fool me,' he sneered. 'It's me that needs protection.'

'And you're going to get it,' Angel said ominously. 'A lifetime of it.'

'He murdered Yvette with Scrap Scudamore's help when he found out she was trying to poison him,' he yelled.

'How do you know that?' Angel snapped.

'My father told me.'

'Yes. He told you by phone after he received the results of the tests from that Harley Street specialist he saw the day Yvette was murdered.'

'Yes.'

'And you hoped he would be pleased if you murdered your stepmother, his wife, for him.'

'No. No. It wasn't like that. He did it and made it look as if it was me.'

Angel shook his head. He gave the tape machine a glance to check that the tape was rolling. Then he turned back to Duncan. He could see the man was struggling to steady his rapid breathing.

'You didn't welcome the arrival of Yvette as your stepmother, did you? Mind you, you wouldn't have wanted anybody, would you? You held a grudge against her from the start, but you always pretended to like her for the sake of your father. Your business wasn't doing too well either, was it? You could have done with a financial leg up when your father announced his upcoming plans to marry Yvette. That would've have been a shock to the system. You must have been livid. And you couldn't keep your resentment from your closest business mate and drinking pal, Scrap Scudamore, could you?'

'He did it. He murdered Yvette and my father helped him!'

Angel pressed on. 'I daresay you dropped it out to him one night in The Feathers — how your father's marriage would greatly reduce your inheritance expectations. I expect Scrap pointed it out to you. And I expect, among other words of wisdom, he indicated what would happen to your inheritance if she fell pregnant! Especially if your father died first! I expect that caused a bit of a flurry when you realized that.'

'No. No. It's not true. It's not true!' he yelled.

Angel ignored him. 'Your business as "fence" to the Scudamores and others has not gone unnoticed by uniformed division. You've been skating on thin ice for some time. Anyway, I'm over running my story a bit. Your father was being poisoned by Yvette because he carelessly killed his friend, Marcus La Touche, who was her father. This was her revenge. As you told me, your father telephoned you on his mobile and told you this immediately after he had been given the results of tests on his stomach conducted by a doctor in Harley Street. He made the call from there just before his driver, Melanie Bright picked him up round the corner in Marylebone Road.'

'No. It was after that. Yesterday, I think it was. Yes.'

'This was a golden opportunity for you. Get rid of Yvette, and if your father found out, get praise from him for showing concern for his safety. Also he wouldn't have given you away to the police. So you enrolled Scrap Scudamore to help you. You knocked up a plan to help you dispose of Yvette; and you agreed to pay him ten thousand pounds. You worked it out that Yvette would be on her own between four o'clock and five o'clock that Friday afternoon. That was after Mr and Mrs Moore had left and before your father arrived back from London. You'd easily be able to gain admission to the Hall. Yvette would let you in. She had no reason to suspect you of any ill will towards her. The alarms and buzzers and the noise of car tracks and feet on the new gravel afforded no protection for her against her "loving" stepson and his accomplice. And it was the easiest thing in the world for you to murder her, undress her and get Scrap Scudamore to take her body up to Western Beck in the dark, dump it, and then destroy her clothes and handbag to effect her complete disappearance. So that's what you did. And Scrap Scudamore took a black plastic bin liner to put her clothes, pearls and handbag in. But Scrap didn't want to take the body out of the Hall starkers, so it was rolled in the carpet, but he was to bring the carpet back and you would've returned it to the hearth. However, in the rush, he accidentally dropped it in Western Beck and it was too wet to return.'

'It's not true,' Duncan snapped.

Angel continued unmoved. 'Well, everything was going nicely for you, and we were completely baffled. Of course, your father was suspect number one and the Scudamores also came into our reckoning. I briefly thought that Scrap Scudamore was guilty of the murder of Yvette. But he hadn't the brains to be a serious contender. He let you down, firstly by not returning the hearthrug, and secondly by not destroying your stepmother's belongings. You may not have been aware that the contents of the bin liner were still in his house, under his bed. Also, when his car had a puncture and he had no spare tyre and he wanted some wheels, he remembered the car key he had seen in Yvette's handbag. He got the key, came up to the Hall, presumably after dark. Probably got a lift from his brother, Scott, and stole the Citroen from the unlocked garage at the back of the Hall. He was actually using it as his runabout. He even drove it to the Can Can Club the night you murdered him. We found it parked in a back street off Bradford Road. That was confirmed when the key was found in his pocket at the mortuary. You slipped up there, Duncan. You should have gone through his pockets.'

Duncan sat staring at Angel, trance like, occasionally shaking his head.

'Up to that point you seemed to have got away with Yvette's murder. However, your relationship with Scrap Scudamore soon soured. I expect he kept on at you about the money you had agreed to pay him. Maybe he'd got as far as blackmailing you. Anyway, he wanted his ten thousand pounds and now wasn't quick enough. It began to dawn on you that you were going to be milked by him for the rest of your life, so you had to think of a way out of the trap. Obviously, you couldn't come to us. There only was one way. You'd got the taste for murder now. And it was beginning to look to you as if you were getting away with it. It hadn't really been that difficult choking Yvette, had it? You thought you could do the same to Scrap. But you would need to disable him first. After all, he was a big man. So you filled him full of booze — the postmortem showed that. *You* remained sober. Well, almost. You needed a certain amount of Dutch courage, didn't you? Later that night you took him round the side of the club and battered him on the back of the head with a brick. Then, when he was on the floor, you leaped on him and choked the last breath out of him. And you didn't let go until he was dead.'

* * *

DS Gawber was hovering in the corridor. He came up to the door when he saw it open.

Angel came out of the interview room wiping his forehead with his handkerchief. He closed the door and waved the cassette at the sergeant.

'It's all here, Ron. Book him. Read him his rights and lock him up. Then come to my office.'

Gawber grinned and then rushed into the interview room.

Angel turned towards his office. He closed the door and dropped the cassette on the desk. He slumped in the chair, still dabbing his face with his handkerchief. Then he opened the desk drawer, found the nicotine chewing gum, tore at the packet and stuffed a strip of gum in his mouth.

A few minutes later, DS Gawber knocked on the door and came in.

'Sit down, Ron. I'm beat. How is Sir Charles?'

Gawber said, 'He seems reconciled to the situation. Melanie Bright picked him up in his car a few minutes ago. He'll be at home by now.'

Angel nodded. 'Good.'

'Would you like some tea, sir?'

'Later. I just want to sit down and have a bit of peace and quiet.'

'Well, can I ask you a question, sir?'

'Of course.'

'How did you know it was Duncan who murdered Lady Yvette?'

Angel smiled. 'Well, I laid a trap, Ron. I knew I was taking a risk. We were never going to be able to prove which one of them was the murderer. We were never going to be able to separate Sir Charles from Duncan. Duncan wanted us originally to think Yvette had simply disappeared! One of the fifteen hundred people who go missing in Britain every year. That's why she was dumped naked in Western Beck. A clumsy attempt at concealing her identity. So when she was found dead and identified, we had to find out *where* she was murdered. Until it was established where she had been murdered there would be an endless number of suspects, with almost as many motives. I couldn't *prove* that Yvette was murdered in the Hall, but I *thought* she was, because of the pantomime with the carpet.'

Gawber nodded.

Angel dabbed his mouth with the handkerchief before continuing. 'If you have to transport a dead body, secretly and in the open air, what better and more innocent way is there, than inside a roll of carpet? Well, I thought she was murdered in the Hall and probably in front of the hearth. And so I planted an unrelated pearl under the grandfather clock in the drawing room near where the carpet had been and then arranged to find it later in Sir Charles's presence. As it later transpired, Yvette *was* murdered there, and, as you would expect, her pearl choker was damaged and loose pearls were presumably dispersed during the actual choking of her. Now, when the pearl I had put there appeared from under the clock, Sir Charles mistakenly thought it was a pearl overlooked in the clearing up after the murder and undressing of Yvette, and he correctly assumed that the murder had taken place right there, on the hearthrug, in Millhouse Hall. And that's what I wanted him to believe. Because of all the security measures, burglar alarms, bells, lights and buzzers, as well as that noisy gravel, nobody could possibly have gained access to the Hall without being seen or heard or both. The murder could only therefore be executed by person or persons Yvette herself chose to admit. The only people she would have admitted (apart from Mr and Mrs Moore and Melanie Bright) were Charles and Duncan. We know that Melanie Bright was with Charles, and that the Moores had gone home. There were, therefore, only two possible people that could have murdered Yvette.'

Gawber said, 'Sir Charles or Duncan.'

Angel nodded. 'Obviously, when Sir Charles saw the pearl, he worked it out. *He* knew the murderer had to be Duncan. There was nobody else, and he reacted accordingly. Naturally, as a good father, his first consideration was the well-being of his son. Not himself! It was *then* that I knew for certain it was Duncan.'

The phone rang. He grunted and reached across the desk. 'Angel.'

It was the WPC on the station switchboard. 'There's a woman by the name of Annabelle Scudamore wants to speak to you, sir.'

Angel's eyebrows shot up. 'Put her on, Constable.'

There was a click.

'Yes? Is that Bella?'

'Yes, you smarmy beggar,' she said. There was a catch in her voice. She sounded near tears. 'I'm in the coach station. I can't talk long. My bus is going to leave any minute. You've got your own way. Now Scrap's gone there's nothing for me down here. All I knows is, I'm not going to be next. I'm going to Galashiels. I'm going to see my daughter. It's my only hope.

I might even stay a while if I'm made welcome. I'm not prepared to stick my neck out for Scott any longer, but don't tell him where I am going. Oh! The driver's arrived. Got to go.'

'Thanks Bella. Goodbye, and good luck!'

'Ah. You always were a smarmy beggar!'

The line went dead.

A big smile slowly dawned across his face. He looked across at the sergeant. 'Annabelle has called in her alibi. She's going back to her little girl and her husband in Scotland. Sensible girl. Now you can go and charge and arrest Scott Scudamore for armed robbery!'

DS Gawber grinned across at him. 'It's our lucky day, sir.'

He stood up to leave.

'Take *two* men with you, Ron,' Angel said sternly. 'I don't want any accidents.'

'Yes, sir,' he replied and went out closing the door.

Angel reached across the desk for the weighty pile of letters and reports. He began to read.

There was a knock at the door. 'Come in,' he growled.

The door opened. Angel looked up.

It was Cadet Ahmed Ahaz. He was not his usual bright self. He came in carrying a small parcel. He was carrying it at arm's length held out in front of him. 'Excuse me, sir,' he said swallowing hard. 'This package has been handed in for you at reception,' he said warily.

Angel pointed to the desktop to indicate he should place it there.

Ahmed lowered it slowly and gently on to the desk, and then quickly stepped back to the door.

The package was about twelve inches by five inches square and wrapped in brown paper that had been used before, and very generously sealed with transparent adhesive tape.

Angel read the words, *Detective Inspector M. Angel*, printed in blue ballpoint pen on an envelope secured to the package by sticky tape. 'What is it? Who's it from?'

Ahmed licked his lips. 'Do you think it's a bomb, sir?'

Angel grinned. 'Nay, don't be daft, lad.'

He picked the package up boldly and shook it. Then he tore the envelope off the wrapping. Inside it was a pink card with a flowered heading. He read the message. It said, *Thank you for everything. From Mr and Mrs Injar Patel.* Angel gave a broad smile. 'Now that's nice, isn't it?'

Ahmed became bolder and advanced to the desk. His smile slowly returned as Angel tore open the package to reveal some printing. It read, *Two hundred filter-tipped Virginia cigarettes.*

THE END

THE JOFFE BOOKS STORY

We began in 2014 when Jasper agreed to publish his mum's much-rejected romance novel and it became a bestseller.

Since then we've grown into the largest independent publisher in the UK. We're extremely proud to publish some of the very best writers in the world, including Joy Ellis, Faith Martin, Caro Ramsay, Helen Forrester, Simon Brett and Robert Goddard. Everyone at Joffe Books loves reading and we never forget that it all begins with the magic of an author telling a story.

We are proud to publish talented first-time authors, as well as established writers whose books we love introducing to a new generation of readers.

We won Trade Publisher of the Year at the Independent Publishing Awards in 2023 and Best Publisher Award in 2024 at the People's Book Prize. We have been shortlisted for Independent Publisher of the Year at the British Book Awards for the last five years, and were shortlisted for the Diversity and Inclusivity Award at the 2022 Independent Publishing Awards. In 2023 we were shortlisted for Publisher of the Year at the RNA Industry Awards, and in 2024 we were shortlisted at the CWA Daggers for the Best Crime and Mystery Publisher.

We built this company with your help, and we love to hear from you, so please email us about absolutely anything bookish at feedback@joffebooks.com.

If you want to receive free books every Friday and hear about all our new releases, join our mailing list here: www.joffebooks.com/freebooks.

And when you tell your friends about us, just remember: it's pronounced Joffe as in coffee or toffee!